WILDERNESS TALES

BY

DAVID OGLE

Wilderness Tales

West Wind Press

All Rights Reserved.

ISBN: 0615973809

ISBN-13: 978-0615973807

Printed in the United States of America

To Melissa,
My Favorite Little Girl

Table of Contents

ALPHONSE THE WOLF

It would be a long winter. Long and difficult. He could feel the chill in the deep places of his heart. The sun was at least two moon cycles away from the end of its southern course and already the skies were churlish and gray. The morning cold lingered and everywhere across the mountainsides the colors had long ago faded. But mostly there was the wind, sometimes shifting through the tops of the big trees, sometimes howling but never absent for long. Unrelenting was the wind with a hard northern edge and Alphonse the Wolf could sense the gravity of the struggle that lay ahead.

He picked his way carefully up the narrow bed of Bear Creek on the eastern side of the Trinity Alps, slowly moving deeper into the Trinity wilderness. He himself knew nothing of these names bestowed upon the land by other creatures. He knew it only as his home, knew every rill and contour, every shadow and sunlit slope, knew everything there was to know about the place but nothing of the names themselves. He had passed all of his fifteen years in this secluded enclave of wilderness, had been born here, mated and fathered many cubs here during his time and he knew the roll and hue of the land as no other creature ever could, knew it all like an imprint on his heart from the big river that flowed down through the valley to the cold lake that lay in the great bowl of shining rock high up in the mountains.

He was almost always comfortable in his natural habitat, but felt uneasy this year in the season of the waning sun. He heard it in the wind and sensed it in the frost flecked morning air. He had seen the signs before, many years ago when he was younger, and he knew. But he was growing older now, was slower and less strong. More importantly perhaps, he had been ill for part of the warm season and had not eaten enough, had not built sufficient stores of fat to carry him through the winter months. He had survived before, had seen the snow creep high upon the trunks of the willow trees down by the river, but he was younger then. Younger and much stronger. Now he was old and far too lean and needed to feed. So he was prowling endlessly in search of food, ceaselessly hunting—desperately trying to nourish himself.

Alphonse's home was the Bear Creek Basin, a small area in a vast wilderness that drained Big Bear Lake and flowed easterly into the headwaters of the Trinity River. The Trinity, in turn, would gather streams from a maze of many smaller basins as it looped its serpentine route to the sea. Bear Creek itself was but a small tendril in an intricate system, but it was the source and while Alphonse knew nothing of the land to the west of the high mountains, he did know that the willows and alders and all the other trees in the lower basin were barren far before their time. So as he crossed over Bear Creek and continued to forage upward, he was anxious—and vaguely fearful.

He was forced to move slowly through the tangle of vegetation in the lower streambed. Alphonse preferred the open areas higher up in the basin where he was able to maneuver with greater ease; nonetheless, the hunting could be good down low. But it was unwieldy terrain, awkward and cumbersome, causing him to spend more energy than he would like. The streambed, to be sure, was a calculated risk, but I am far too lean, he thought to himself, much too lean for a long and difficult winter season and I need to eat.

Often he would look up toward a sun that was sliding further to the south with each passing day; and he listened to the wind, the unceasing wail of the wind. He knew that he must replenish his reservoirs of fat or he would most likely die; must conserve and ration his energy, for it was his most precious possession. He desperately needed to nourish himself and so had been pulling his heavy body through the brush and bramble for several weeks now, back and forth between the boulders and fallen trees, clawing through the clutter of the lower streambed, endlessly searching for food.

But it was difficult. The moon was full when he began and now was nearly full again and during that time he had barely fed at all, a few squirrels and nothing more in one full cycle of the moon as the season of cold and snow began to settle in; lean had turned to bone and he began to despair for his chances as autumn slowly slipped away. And still he kept foraging upward, steadfast in the hunt but growing ever weaker in the fading light of the encroaching winter.

Then one cold and stillborn morning in the dim light of a gibbous moon, he spied a yearling fawn. The young deer was standing motionless, frozen on the forest edge, probing for danger. Listening and sniffing the air. She would bolt at any sound that was out of place, Alphonse knew, any movement anywhere and she would flee. And she was all alone, or so it seemed—at least the mother was nowhere to be seen. Perhaps she had died or somehow been scared away or perhaps anything. It was not important. The fawn was unattended and hopelessly vulnerable.

She moved forward slowly, step by step, eyes like mirrors in the early light, searching everywhere. She would hesitate at every step, head flicking from side to side, scanning for some rupture in the rhythm of the pattern of the forest. But mainly she listened; listened for the slightest sound that shouldn't be. But there was only the rustle of the wind sifting through the trees and the ripple of the braiding of the stream, nothing more, and so she slowly continued moving down toward the water. She was taut with fear, quivering and desperately alone, but also very thirsty. And so she kept creeping closer to the water's edge along the strand of the Bear Creek as Alphonse silently watched.

He was slouched down low on his rear haunch, motionless in the darkness of an alder thicket. He would wait, must wait, in silence until she started to drink. He lay very close to where she would be standing and would snatch her by surprise; must pounce and grab her where she stood or be denied, for he would surely lose her in the chase—had not a chance to bring her down if she should start to run. It was a good and rare opportunity, a large meal for an aging wolf and as he lay there in the dampness and early frost midst the tangle of alders, he knew he could not fail.

When he was younger and less mature, he had often sprung too soon and scared his prey away. But he was older now and less impulsive, was able to control his ancient instincts; and so he patiently abided. But it was not easy. The lack of nourishment had weakened him and his right rear haunch began to tremble uncontrollably. Still, he remained breathless and silent and since the trembling caused no audible sound, the fawn continued to move forward, innocent and unaware. Weary to exhaustion, muscles aching everywhere, Alphonse drew from the wisdom of many years and forced himself to wait, knowing full well that the next few minutes would most likely determine whether he lived or died.

The yearling had cleared the forest's edge by now and was standing in the open space near the margin of the creek. Still cautious as she drew closer to the stream, she stopped to test the air. And listened. Searched the thickets once again, checked the sprawl of streamside boulders, sniffed and flicked her head from side to side. And listened. But there was nothing to be heard save the rush and tumble of the water. And still she paused and listened several minutes more, ears pricked, every muscle tensed for flight. Finally, satisfied that all was well, she proceeded tenuously down on toward the water's edge and began to drink.

Alphonse remained silent and ready in the darkened enclave of the alder thicket several yards from where the fawn was lapping at the water. His body was trembling throughout by now and he could barely control his position; how simple, he thought to himself, it was to do these things when I was younger. And how difficult it has become. Nonetheless, he persevered, continued waiting and watching, hunched down low, eyes fixed on the advancing fawn.

The yearling, as Alphonse knew she would, had become careless with the drinking of the water. She would from time to time lift her head and briefly listen, but would quickly return to the stream once again. And with each cycle of listening and drinking she became less attentive to the undertow of the surrounding forest, became more and more confident that she was safe from harm.

He would strike while she satisfied her thirst, when her head was down and she was least aware. He lay silent along the frozen banks of the Bear Creek carefully gauging the moment, then sprang suddenly forward, exploding from the alder thicket like a coiled snake and tried to bring her down at once. He lunged upward and out with all the strength his lean and aching body would allow and tried to knock her off her feet. But the yearling deer was much too quick. She must have heard the snap of an alder bough as he broke from the thicket and instinctively leapt straight up and bolted. He wasn't even close as she bounded easily and gracefully away into the darkened entrails of the forest. Alphonse desperately gave chase, but it was useless.

Then unexpectedly, and it was truly rare that such a thing would happen, the yearling slipped and fell as her hooves became ensnared in the underbrush of a nearby willow grove. She immediately tried to gain her feet, but Alphonse was on her at the instant. The silence of the basin was momentarily interrupted by the sounds of the struggle as the fawn squealed and bleated, hooves flailing away against the dampened soil. But she had no chance, not in the least, and it ended quickly.

Alphonse feasted joyously that morning, engorged himself as the early light began to filter down through the forest canopy. He wasted nothing, leaving only a pile of scattered bones and hair, devoured the fawn with an ardor that could only spring from the deepest of hungers. Then, as the full light of mid morning began to spread across the forest floor, he curled himself into a ball and fell asleep, warm and comfortable for the first time in many days. But it was a dark and troubled sleep, restless and turning, for he knew that he had moved too slowly toward the kill; knew he had been lucky and feared in his heart for what lay ahead.

For several weeks he worked his way up the streambed of Bear Creek basin. At times he would wander off into the hills, but mainly he hunted close to the water. It was his plan to reach the big lake before the heavy snows arrived and then move slowly back down, feeding all the while, retracing his route until he once again crossed over into the valley of the Trinity where he could safely pass the winter. But always he needed to keep on the front edge of the snowline or he would be lost.

Food was scarce everywhere in the Bear Creek drainage in the winter season, but up high among the wind whipped rock and treeless mountainsides, it was impossible. A few birds survived up there perhaps, a few insects, but little else. It was fierce in the upper basin in the heart of the winter season, deadly and unforgiving and in the mere passing of a quarter moon he could be isolated and buried. He nonetheless surmised he still had time to reach the lake before the onset of the big storms, time to feed upon the marmots and scattering of other rodents that made their home midst the piles of scree that fanned out across the slopes of the big mountain; but as he scanned the horizon he could see that the clouds were growing ever darker, scudding lower with each passing day. And the wind seemed never to cease.

The snows had not yet begun however and he did feel stronger than before. Still, he was too lean. The yearling deer had provided much needed sustenance, to be sure, but he had eaten little since—a few ground squirrels and nothing more. Nonetheless, as he moved ever higher he was able to travel with greater ease. The land began to open up as the alder thickets and willow groves from down below gave way to grassy meadows. In the upper reaches of the basin, the forests thinned and everywhere there was more light, more space to roam and his confidence began to return as he scampered across the rock strewn hillsides, stretching out, gliding at will across the open terrain.

The pure joy of being in the high basin provided a momentary lull of pleasure and his thoughts strayed back toward his youth when he had roamed the Bear Creek area with his lifelong mate Antoinette. Their union had yielded many cubs and together they had prowled tirelessly and fearlessly throughout the hills and streams of the Trinity wilderness, often ranging great distances in search of food. As a team they moved unchallenged through the land, hunting and feasting at will, for they had no enemies. They were too quick and too strong to tempt the bear and while the creature who walked on two legs could be troublesome—he seemed strange and vaguely dangerous to them both—he rarely ventured into their territory. Antoinette herself was tenacious and fast for a female, even wise in her way he thought; they were as one and it had been good with her. But she was gone now.

It had been seven cycles of the seasons, he remembered, since she had snapped both her front legs in a long fall from a boulder field high up on a cliff near the big lake. It was in the season of the waning sun, the same as now, and she had slowly starved, whimpering softly through the long days as she waited out her time. Alphonse nurtured her throughout, brought her what food he could find, but it was hopeless. He had howled his sorrow through the deepening nights while he watched her slowly fade, his grief echoing out across the starlit mountainsides for one full cycle of the moon as he tended to her needs. He stayed until she had finally died and then descended, mournfully weeping, down through the early snows and on into the valley where he passed the loneliest winter of all.

He missed her, wished her by his side again. But all of that was in the past; he was alone now and growing old, bracing for the onslaught of another winter. The days were never warm this time of year as the sun slipped ever lower into the southern sky. Always there was a chill upon the air and the nights were long and forbidding in their coldness. Already the ridgelines were powdered with freshly fallen snow and as he moved higher into the basin the wind became his constant, relentless companion.

It was the realm of shining rock and lichen splashed boulders, of shattered crest lines and fractured granite walls, all of it grand and beautiful in its way one could suppose, but Alphonse sensed only the hostility of the place and knew he must not delay. But for now he allowed himself a few hours of pleasure as he romped across the glistening slabs of rock. He had struggled mightily in the congestion of the lower basin, had felt constrained by the closeness of the terrain, but now he could ramble to his heart's bidding and so he did, gamboling and bounding across the open spaces to near exhaustion, unwisely burning his meager stores of energy, unable, nonetheless, to restrain his natural instincts. Then he lay down for the night and entered into a deep and peaceful sleep.

He awakened the next morning and immediately proceeded upward, clearing the rim of the big lake as the sun was beginning to rotate in from the eastern sky. The lake itself sat in a large, nearly circular bowl and its dark waters seemed to him to be unusually calm. The shrubs and low bushes at the lake's strandline were already dusted in several inches of fresh snow and the air was cold. The sun continued to rise, but the sky remained dark. He searched the horizon and there was no trace of light anywhere, only the darkness tinged by the dull and distant glow of an obscure sun. Never before had he seen the sky so black in the face of a breaking dawn; never before had he seen the waters of the lake so quiescent in the early hours of a mountain sunrise.

There was an ominous feel in the air and he immediately began to fear for the worst. And then, almost without warning, the wind exploded, came pouring down the mountainsides as if some large, celestial dam had suddenly burst; came screaming across the lake and whipped the tranquil waters into a froth. The suddenness of it all was astonishing to him. Never have I seen the wind like this, he thought to himself, never have I seen the sky so dark this time of day. He knew at once he must act, knew he could not waver for a second and so set out to seek some kind shelter, anything at all, as the snows commenced to fall.

Everything was happening quickly now, everything began to rage and spin all about him. It was dark and cold and the wind drove the chill down into his very core. Alphonse knew that his life could be measured in the passage of mere minutes if he remained out in the open, knew that he needed to find some kind of windbreak, anything, as quickly as possible and so he forced himself to keep moving, forced himself to keep stumbling through the darkness and cold and slashing snow. It was a desperate search in desperate circumstances, but it was all he could really do—all he truly knew how to do. And so he lowered his head and pushed forward into the howling winds.

Then quite suddenly and miraculously he brushed across a large boulder that had become wedged between two trees, forming a natural, cave like enclosure. He felt it rather than saw it and at once slipped beneath the protection of the large rock, huddling meekly into a small corner of the cramped space. He then curled into a ball beneath the boulder and prepared to wait it out; but it was a bad situation and he knew it. As the storm began to roar across the lake with ever increasing virulence, engulfing everything in its way, he tried to fall asleep; but he was trembling from the cold and sleep did not come easily.

It was the worst of storms, lasting seven days and seven nights without ebbing in the slightest. The wind ran free through it all, rarely waning, driving the snow into every crack and crevice, smothering everything in its path. The deepening drifts buried everything along the shoreline and pushed into every corner of the basin. Only the lake, as yet unfrozen, remained distinct, appearing as some huge black hole in a vast expanse of white. And through it all Alphonse lay entombed beneath the boulder, twisting and turning through the long days, sleeping but fitfully, chilled to the marrow and growing weaker with every passing day.

Then on the dawn of the eighth morning the wind and snow stopped as suddenly as they had begun. The sun rose into an ice blue sky and an eerie silence fell across the basin. Seven days and seven nights, like some phantom from the dark side it had ripped through the upper reaches of the Bear Creek and now was gone. Alphonse had been buried in the darkness for the duration and had lost all sense of time, but the faint glow of light filtering down through the layers of snow informed him that it was over. He could not tell precisely how much time had passed since he had crawled beneath the boulder; certainly it was much longer than any storm he had ever known before. But he knew that it was over now and so began to claw his way back up through the snow and into the open basin.

Finally, after several tedious hours, he broke through the surface and dragged himself into the brilliance of the midday sun. It was at once wondrous and frightening as the blinding light shimmered off the snow from every angle, everywhere. Everything was swathed in white save the dark hole of the big lake. As he drew the scene into focus, he saw that the entire basin had been transformed into a cold, glistening, cauldron of ice and snow. All of it, every rock and tree, every shrub and willow bush lay submerged beneath a rolling veil of white.

Only the steepest of the granite walls and the lake itself remained untouched; all else was buried deep below the silent snows, a world apart, sealed off from heaven and earth alike. Alphonse knew that he could not hesitate, innately sensed he had lost much of his strength and knew he must make his way down toward the lower stream bed as soon as possible. Nonetheless he lingered for several minutes more, transfixed by the grandeur of the scene that lay before him; for it was like nothing he had ever seen before.

He was, however, very much aware that he needed to escape from the open terrain of the high basin, knew he must strike for the big trees down below where there would be less drifting. Alphonse, of course, was unburdened with abstract ruminations of any sort, knew nothing of his own mortality, nothing of the inevitable termination of his existence through natural attrition, but he did know of dying from other causes—knew that he could starve. Or freeze. He had seen it happen to others many times before and was well acquainted with the face and fact of death and so knew that he must not tarry.

He briefly ran his gaze across the gleaming basin, shook himself several times in an effort to shed the wetness, then plunged boldly ahead down toward the forest. But it was hard. He could only move by lunging forward through the heavy snow—lunge and sink, lunge and sink and with every cycle he grew ever weaker. He was cold and trembling now, a ragged, aging wolf plowing desperately through the deep snows. And it was exhausting.

He pushed forward for many hours, unthinking, numbed with cold and moving by instinct alone. Lunge and sink, lunge and sink but the forest's edge remained always in the distance, never seeming to draw any closer. The shadows were lengthening now as the sun began to sink beneath the western horizon. This was the final day of its southern journey and its arc was low. The brilliance of midday had begun to fade into the soft blue of early evening and there was a hush across the basin. The only sound to be heard was the lunging and thrashing of a solitary wolf as he struggled down through the fathomless snows.

Finally he stopped and looked up toward the darkening rim of an ash gray sky. The day was on the wane and he was very tired. I must rest, he thought to himself, I must conserve my strength. I need to rest. And so without delay he scraped away a small enclosure beneath the surface of the newly fallen snow and lay down. At once, it seemed, he was embraced by the profoundest sense of well being, was at once immersed in a sudden flush of warmth and pleasure. How strange, he mused, as his mind began to drift back into the past, how warm and comfortable this is. How very pleasant. He lifted his eyes one last time toward the distant forest, then tucked his head down between his paws and settled into a deep and peaceful sleep. And then the silence was absolute.

MELISSA THE LIONESS

It would be a long night. Long and difficult. The shadows had begun to lengthen by now and the sun was slowly sinking beneath the western rim of the equatorial sky. The undulating heat of late afternoon hovered like a shroud above the endless expanse of open savanna land; merciless was the heat in this the summer season, constant and unrelenting. As always, an ominous silence prevailed at this hour of the day, broken only by the low drone of the insane flies as they fed upon the dung heaps that lay strewn across the sun baked grasslands. The indolence of early twilight permeated everywhere, hung like a pestilence over the great plains of East Africa as Melissa the lioness girded for the struggle that lay ahead.

She lay wounded to the marrow, the length of her rear haunch opened to the bone. The flow of blood had finally begun to slow, had diminished to a trickle, but the gash was deep and wide. She could not see the wound of course, it was hidden from view; but she knew, could sense the severity of it instinctively. And she could see the shallow pools of blood that shimmered crimson beneath the remorseless African sun and she knew the blood was her own. And now with the approaching darkness the numbness had begun to fade and the serious pain was beginning to settle in, dull at first but increasing with every pulse of her heart. The pain would grow, she knew, would intensify as it spread out from the dark mass at the base of the wound and she was anxious about it; but mainly she feared for the coming of the night.

Melissa had hunted the grasslands of East Africa for all her life and had never feared for anything, was a commanding presence in the land where she dwelled, acknowledging no enemy or foe save the creature who walked upright on two legs. And although he could be unpredictable, unreasonable and cruel at his worst it seemed to her, she had learned to avoid him. But it was a teeming, predatory place, perilous and unforgiving, where she had nonetheless managed to survive for seven years without serious injury or mishap. Until the fall.

It had happened while she was resting on the lower limb of a massive Baobab tree, spread out in languid repose, when suddenly and without warning the branch had snapped. She had plunged earthward abruptly, landing heavily on the jagged spar of a large boulder. The razor edge of the rock had slashed easily through the tendon and muscle of her powerful rear haunch; had split it open like a scalpel and left her helpless.

It was the worst of circumstances and she knew it. Wounded and defenseless, weakened by loss of blood, she would be easy prey for all those creatures who hunted in the shadows of the moon. She was by nature a nocturnal hunter herself, had often preyed upon the wounded and weak and she knew that she would be a nourishing meal for any one of them; an unexpected feast. But she was aware, as well, that they would approach with caution, all of them, all the scavengers and predators of the East African plains who prowled the darkness in search of food, would proceed with due trepidation; for she was a large cat, a fierce and determined adversary and she had earned their respect. So in spite of the loss of blood and growing weakness, in spite of the fact that the pain was causing everything to blur now into a golden, dusky haze and the skies were beginning to spin wildly above her, she realized that they must wait until nightfall, comprehended well that she had three hours, maybe four, before the onset of the assaults.

The pain had become uncomfortable now, was deepening, and she anguished from it. The flies, thousands of them, had begun to feed upon the open wound, were swarming to the gash in her rear haunch, legions of them rising up from the dust. And it was a torment for her, the pain and constant drone of the flies, the weakness and nausea, the solitude—all of it an affliction beyond anything she had ever known before. A cold and abiding fear began to well up from the deep places of her heart, a portent of misfortune so strong that it caused her to openly tremble. She wailed for awhile, softly and without shame, a plaintive cry of frustration that was swept away by the winds of early evening; then she breathed deeply and began to patiently prepare for the mortal encounter that lay ahead.

First she tried to lick the wound clean, straining her head to the rear as far as she could; but it was useless. Then she rolled from side to side, as best she could, in the dust and dung of the dry earth in an effort to smother the flies, but it was useless as well. And so she rested for awhile, tried to regain some strength and perspective, contemplated the situation and slowly began to measure her chances. She glanced up toward a horizon that was quickly fading to dusk as the great orb of the equatorial sun began to rotate rapidly to the west. Melissa had witnessed similar scenes before, had seen other creatures—zebras, cheetahs, wildebeests and many others—maimed and desperate, suffering terribly in the heat and isolation of the empty savanna, hopelessly vulnerable as they waited the onset of darkness; had watched as they were ripped apart by bands of ravening predators, their bones ultimately picked clean by the vultures.

She was aware that if she remained out in the open she would be savaged, knew she must seek a stronghold, some sort of protection, or she would surely perish. But as she gazed out across the broad sweep of empty savanna, there was nothing, nothing but the slow rhythm of the grasses swaying softly in the early twilight, nothing but the ominous aspect of the deepening East African sky. And then she remembered the Baobab tree from which she had fallen and realized at once that it was her only chance, her only resource; knew instinctively that she must make her way to the base of that tree if she were to survive. And it would be there, beneath its gnarled canopy, where for better or for worse she would make her stand. But she had to reach the tree before nightfall, must not linger or she would be lost. The hulking Baobab with its massive trunk was her only chance, no doubt, but she must not tarry.

It was perhaps twenty yards, no more, to the foot of the tree, but she knew that it would be her longest journey ever. She was aware that her right rear leg and haunch would be useless and knew, as well, from the sound of snapping bone when she landed that she had fractured her left hip. And so she came to realize as she lay there in the lengthening shadows, desolate and apart, that she would need to use her front legs and paws to drag herself to the base of the Baobab. But it would not be easy.

Melissa was a mature lioness, thick and heavy through the shoulders and girth, weighing well over six hundred pounds, and it would be an ordeal. Her front legs and paws were evolved for balance and control, for tearing flesh and stripping bones, were deft and efficient for their purpose but singularly ill designed for the impending task. And while her shoulders were indeed powerful, the source of her mobility lay in her rear haunch, now shattered and flaccid and drumming with pain. It would be an agony for her, a grim and fearsome passage and she shuddered at the thought of it.

The sky by now had begun to fade toward deep twilight and she knew she could not delay. But first she stretched the muscles of her shoulders and upper torso, rolled her neck from side to side, then lifted her head and from deep within unleashed a roar that caused the very heavens to rumble. She was being watched, she knew, and so she issued a warning, a challenge, to each and all within her range that she would not yield easily; informed all the creatures of the grasslands now lurking in wait for the waning of the day's light that she would not go quietly. With one fierce and defiant roar proclaimed her resolve and then turned to face the struggle that lay before her.

She gradually rotated her large body until she was facing the base of the tree; then she slowly began dragging herself forward. She would roll to one side, reach out with the opposite paw and pull herself ahead. Shifting from one side to the other, rolling and dragging, sinking her paws as best she could into the hard baked savanna, she clawed her way toward the Baobab. But it was tedious and painful. And ever so slow. Inch by inch, measure by measure, she moved forward as the last, lingering arc of the evening sun slid beneath the horizon. Digging and clawing, growling with pain from time to time, struggling mightily, until at last, as the faint light of dusk finally gave way to the deep shadows of late evening, she arrived at the foot of the big tree.

The darkness was everywhere now and the wind had dropped. The sun had slipped far below the rim of the western sky, but the heat of midday persisted and would surely last into early morning. An uncommon silence had spread across the grasslands that night as the normal prowl of nocturnal activity deferred to the patient vigil of the scavengers. There was a foreboding in the East African air; it could be felt rather than seen or heard, but its presence was palpable—an augury of death and struggle that hung over the land like a promise. The hunters of the night were lying in wait, of that she was certain, gauging the hour, salivating with anticipation she supposed. And Melissa could do nothing more than lie there and bear with it, silently moaning, exhausted from the effort to reach the tree, could do nothing more than patiently abide, knowing that the assaults would soon begin.

They would be hyenas with their low haunches and sloping backs; she had seen it before. The loathsome spotted hyena, odious and vile to her, legendary, hereditary enemy of all lions everywhere; and they would come at her in large numbers, eight or ten to a pack and maybe more. It was rare that the hyena would attack such a big cat, even one who was seriously wounded; the power and quickness of a mature lioness were far too much for them.

But the savanna of East Africa had been desiccated by five years of unmerciful drought, five years of famine and starvation and the hyenas had become emboldened as the parched land swallowed up their own in ever increasing numbers. They were far more aggressive now, she knew, far more daring, and they would be unrestrained in their efforts to feed. There were other night scavengers, other predators as well—leopards and jackals and other lions—but it would be the spotted hyena, she was sure, the deadly spotted, frenzied and crazed with hunger, who would come for her that night.

As she lay there resting, gathering what strength remained, her thoughts drifted back to an earlier time, one other time so very long ago, or so it seemed to her now, when she had been forced to engage the enemy. It was during the season of the rains, in her fourth year, when she was nurturing three new born cubs. The father of her children, an aging, apathetic male, had abandoned her, as was the habit of all her mating partners every year. Only this time, as nature would have it, a young male, ambitious and proud, had wandered into the territory and staked his claim.

The older cat, by now weary and indifferent, offered scant resistance and the young lion wasted little time in asserting his dominance, began stalking her young cubs at once, hunting them down one by one. It was his intention to kill them all so that no genetic trace of his predecessor would survive, no threat from the past could ever again rise up to challenge his reign. It was an instinctive response, primordial, and no lioness alive could ever hope to deny a young, virile male who was intent on imposing his will, had not a chance; but Melissa was determined to try.

She would protect the strongest and sacrifice the other two. It was her only option; all that she could really do. She concealed all three, but stayed close to one, an energetic male who was larger and more agile than the other two. The intruder began to stalk the cubs early one evening in the dim light of a crescent moon, cautious and methodical, slowly sweeping through the high grass. Confident unto arrogance, he hunted them down with instinctive precision, determined to erase every scent and vestige of the senescent patriarch, patiently combing, testing the air, sniffing and listening.

The first two, both females, were easy for him however; frightened and frantic, they began to immediately mew and yelp for their mother, quickly betraying their positions. He was on them like a bolt from the heavens, pounced instantly and snapped their necks with one swift crunch of his powerful jaws—then proceeded to eat them one at a time. Melissa watched from a distance, distraught and dismayed, weeping silently in frustration as she witnessed the young male devour her children; but she did not charge, rather held her position and waited.

He delayed not a second, licked his lips and then turned toward Melissa. He made a low, guttural sound, poignant and sinister, the unadorned challenge of an adolescent lion in all his pride and prowess; and then began to slowly circle her. She followed his every movement as the circle tightened, tracked his every step, feigning an attack now and then, roaring her defiance from time to time, as he slowly closed the distance. He was unmoved by her threats, however, was absolutely committed to the destruction of the young cub as he moved ever closer, unwavering, closer yet, until Melissa was at last forced to respond.

She lunged suddenly, went for his neck as was her instinct, but he brushed her to the side with one crushing sweep of his huge paw, then charged, swatted her about at will for awhile and then pushed her away, roaring with imperious disdain as she was at last constrained to flee her ground. She watched from afar as he swooped down on the terrified cub, snatched him by the neck and ate him. She remembered it all like an imprint on her soul, recalled every mournful detail and the sadness returned as the anguish of it all washed back across her memory. And she wept.

But nearly three cycles of the seasons had passed since then and while she lamented the death of her cubs, lamented her helplessness during those final few minutes, it was all in the past. She was alone now, wounded and weak, bracing for the onslaught of the hyenas and feeling her heart fill with the same dread that she had felt those many years ago. Nonetheless, she began to prepare for the long night ahead as the howling and yipping of the pack finally commenced.

It was a strange and doleful sound this wail of the spotted hyena, a melancholy, desolate sound that floated through the African darkness like the cry of a thousand phantoms. It would hang for an instant in the slow heat of the empty savanna and then trail off into the distance—a shrill and penetrating squall that caused Melissa to fear for her life. Caused her to wonder, then, if she could ever survive the encroaching night.

The skies had deepened into ebony by now and the heavens of East Africa began to fill with stars. The wind was quiet and the silence nearly complete save for the constant shrieking of the hyenas. From the sound of it, this pack tonight was smaller than usual, six to eight animals, no more, but their fervor seemed boundless and so she knew it would be difficult. The hyenas had begun to move out from the bush, she could tell, were beginning to dart back and forth, hurtling and spinning everywhere in all directions, as was their habit—working themselves into a frenzy, aroused by the smell of blood and their terrible hunger as they began to slowly circle closer.

Melissa was a predator of the night as well, a hunter fully accustomed to the darkness, and so her vision was tuned to the absence of light. She could easily discern the ambitious advance of the more aggressive members of the pack, could easily perceive the glint of their eyes flash wild in the rising glow of the moonlight, tracked the gleam in their eyes as they scrambled around feverishly, yelping and squealing. Melissa by now felt no pain as a massive release of adrenaline surged through her body. It was nature's gift to all creatures everywhere and while she knew nothing of such things, knew nothing of her body's biological response, she could feel her muscles begin to tense involuntarily, sensed a resurgence of strength; experienced a heightened awareness and so instinctively began to gather herself for the impending assault.

She had maneuvered her rear haunch so that it was lodged firmly against the base of the big tree, thereby providing ample protection for her wounded rear flank. She then faced out toward the open grasslands, risen up on her front paws, alert and fully primed to defend her life by any means necessary. The hyenas were leaping and spinning everywhere now, skirling and howling, snarling mindlessly into the darkness. It all appeared to be random and dissolute, a formless blur of movement for its own sake, but Melissa knew better. It was a planned confusion, a diversionary tactic that would permit one or two of the larger females to lead the attack.

And they would be females, of that she was certain, for the clan of the hyena was a matriarchy, a formidable sisterhood in which female members were dominant. The lowly males existed solely for the purpose of breeding, were virtual pariahs within their own societies, devoid of status or authority. And so it was that she glimpsed through the dim glow of the ascending moon two large, mature females circling ever closer, tails erect and teeth bared, screaming and squalling, nearly febrile in their fury; poised for their initial charge.

The moment burst upon her suddenly as the two of them lunged simultaneously for her throat. She rose up instantly, emitting a mighty roar, rose up in all her leonine majesty and ripped open the under belly of one, eviscerated her with one fearful swat of her front paw; laid it out useless and dying, squirming on the ground in front of her. The other one, however, managed to lock her powerful jaws into Melissa's right shoulder, sinking her teeth deep into the sinew.

Melissa reacted at once, began to violently shake her heavy torso from side to side, up and down, thrashing about furiously, doing all that she could to dislodge the squalling female. Writhing and twisting, tossing back and forth she desperately tried to shake the frenzied hyena, drew upon every resource of strength she possessed in an effort to shed the demented creature who was by now foaming from the mouth and nearly delirious. Undaunted, however, was this large female, stubborn and unyielding; it was a desperate struggle between two desperate foes, a mortal encounter between ancient enemies and it was fierce.

Then, with one great twisting surge she tossed her, caused the hyena to release her grip, then seized her from the air and slammed her to the ground. She was on it in an instant, snatching its neck into her jaws and suffocating her. The helpless female squealed and wailed, a high, whining sound that cut through the warm, dry African air like a siren; she lurched and pitched about for a while, struggled desperately to free herself, and then fell silent.

Melissa at once dropped the dead body to the ground, rose up on her front haunch and bellowed her conquest for all to hear, unleashed a deep roar that boomed across the darkened grasslands like a roll of thunder. Roared and bellowed until she was hoarse, for she knew that the rest of the pack had been watching, had witnessed the destruction of the most valiant amongst them and would surely be intimidated by the ferocity of this wounded lioness. She roared her defiance once again, one last time, then settled back down onto one side and began to consider her possibilities.

But she was spent. The one female who had clamped into her shoulder had been strong and tenacious and Melissa was numb with exhaustion; weary to her depths and trembling throughout the length of her wounded body. The pain, momentarily stilled by the rush of adrenaline, had begun to return and was an enduring distraction, an annoyance that would only continue to spread. Nonetheless, she knew it was not over, knew the remaining hyenas would regroup and once again mount an attack. Only this time the entire pack would come at her, all of them all at once in one furious surge. Melissa believed the Hyena to be cowardly at its core and so they would wait awhile in an effort to bolster their courage, but they would be coming; of that she was certain. And she knew she must somewhere find the strength to once again rise up and confront them or she would surely die. But it was not easy. Lying there beneath the Baobab as the whining and yipping of the pack echoed through the darkness, she felt profoundly tired. And hopelessly alone.

The heat had diminished by now and a slight chill hung in the night air. The broad savanna glowed in the pale light of a gibbous moon as it rotated ever higher into the infinite African sky. The branches of the great tree cast their twisted shadows across the space where Melissa lay, solitary and trembling. It was late into early morning and the night sounds permeated everywhere— the cawing of the vultures, the roars and squeals from assorted distant struggles, the piercing laughter of the baboons, all of it a natural and recurrent cycle of life on the East African plain.

Eerie and forbidding were the night cries as they rose and fell across the savanna lands; but this night Melissa could hear nothing but the yelping of the hyenas as they began to stir themselves into another frenzy. She tried to rest, tried to conserve her strength, but it was difficult. Her heart was pumping wildly and the pain was surging everywhere now, a deep, paralyzing pain that caused her eyes to fill with tears. Nonetheless, she tried to rest.

The hyenas had begun to gather, preparing for their final rush. And it would be their final effort, she knew; with two strong females lying dead at her feet, no doubt the two dominant females of the clan, the remainder of the pack was much more circumspect, much more tentative. And while the yelping and yowling were more fevered than ever, they seemed slightly more reluctant, were closing the distance, to be sure, but ever so slowly.

Hyenas were mainly eaters of carrion and the sight of two dead females lying there beneath the Baobab in ever expanding pools of their own blood was a shock to them. Two preeminent members of their family destroyed by the power of a wounded lioness was like nothing they had ever seen before. But they were starving and their young were starving, all of them dying off in fearful numbers, and so they circled ever closer while Melissa waited, exhausted beyond anything she could have ever imagined. Too tired to even raise her head.

They came at her all at once, as she knew they would, with no warning. It was in the early hours of the morning beneath the sallow glow of a waning moon; a pallid half-light washed across the plains and the air was still. It was like some dark force rising up from the dim reaches of a distant abyss, like a dream, as a frenzy of blurred silhouettes besieged her from all sides. The assault was fervid and chaotic—they rushed her all at once, all five of them, snarling, foam flying from their nostrils, frantic in their bloodlust; came at her with a ferocity that could only have been spawned from the deepest sense of desperation.

Melissa was exhausted to the marrow—miserable and grieved beyond anything she had ever known before—and while she knew nothing of dying as a natural inevitability of her existence, knew nothing of natural mortality and so assumed she would live forever if she survived the assault, she did know that her life could be measured, at this precise instant, by her capacity and will to respond in kind.

They exploded on her from all directions, screaming and yipping, nearly rabid in their fervor. Two of them struck directly for the wounded flank, one for her underbelly and the other two straight for the throat. But she wheeled on all of them all at once, torqueing and twisting, flailing away with both paws, rotating her powerful upper torso violently from side to side. The two who went for her neck plunged unmercifully into the heart of her fury; one she swatted to the side with her forepaw, shattered her ribs and sent her off whimpering and useless. The other she batted away with a crushing blow to the head. It was a young female and she cried out in terror as her head split open, a high, puling sound of instant death as she tumbled lifeless to the ground.

The other three didn't have a chance; confused by all the rapid movement and dismayed by the sudden rout of their brethren, they made a few tentative feints, rose up on their rear haunches and howled, but had not the heart for it. Melissa the lioness, valiant and undeterred, was rocking and roaring now, sweeping furiously from side to side, proclaiming her authority for all to see. The three postured for a brief while, simulated a few attacks, pretended to do something or other and then suddenly spun and fled, whining and bawling, as they slunk off into the sanctuary of the low bush.

Melissa bellowed her triumph, a booming, rasping roar that rolled out across the grasslands and rose up into the skies. And then she collapsed; lay there silent and motionless for a long while. Absolutely exhausted. The low sun of morningtide had begun to rotate in from the east and the heat was on the rise. The moon had faded by now as the savanna lands once again began to stir to life, but she was numb to it all; prostrate and bone weary she simply wished to rest for awhile. Wished only that and nothing more.

She knew she had prevailed, knew that the hyenas would dare not attack again. And while she could glimpse from time to time the gleam of fang and flash of eye from one or another of the predators still lurking in the shadows, she knew that they would all accede to the approaching dawn. And she was aware, above all else, that she would survive; needed only to await the arrival of various of her brethren who would escort her back into the more secluded enclaves of the high bush where she would once again be safe.

For now, however, she would rest, would pause and let her damaged body begin to repair itself. She glanced up briefly toward a horizon that was shimmering now in the full light of an ascending sun, breathing deeply then in an effort to calm her pounding heart. The pain was still with her, but she was unmindful, was conscious only of a sudden flush of warmth and pleasure that flowed upward and out across her broken body. Her response had been unfaltering, she knew, swift and deadly and she was pleased with it all. The journey back home would be long and slow, no doubt, for her wounds were grievous and she had been ravaged by the rigors of battle.

Nonetheless, she was very much satisfied, paid but passing heed to the discomfort of her circumstance, euphoric in the redolence of the conquest. As she prepared to await the arrival of her family and friends, she gazed out once more across the endless savanna lands, out across the great expanse of the East African plain that was her home, confident that she would for now and forever remain the dominant force in the land where she lived. Then she tucked her head down between her paws, softly sighed and closed her eyes, settling at long last into a deep and peaceful sleep.

NATHAN THE CAT

It would be a long journey. Long and difficult. Nathan the Cat knew he was far from home, sensed that he had been set adrift in an alien land. He could feel it in the dryness of the early morning air and could taste it in the water; could see it everywhere all about him. He was at once bewildered and beguiled as he gazed up toward the great walls of Zion Canyon, shimmering golden now in the silent hush of a desert sunrise. It was, all of it, so very strange to him and while he was enchanted by the grandeur of the place he nonetheless understood the gravity of his circumstance, comprehended well that he had been abandoned and was a long way from his home in San Francisco.

Nathan was a city cat, sophisticated and wise in his fashion he supposed, but thoroughly unaccustomed to the ways of the wilderness. He was, he had always assumed, a valued and respected member of an affluent San Francisco family, the Sanfords; there was Nathan, Marisol the daughter and Constance and Harold the parents. They all lived together in relative harmony in the Pacific Heights section of that city. Constance and Harold, both lawyers, were financially secure and quite willing to provide Nathan with a comfortable existence, cushy and posh if the truth be known, especially considering that Nathan was not a pure bred and had been purchased principally as an amusement for Marisol.

They had all been vacationing in Zion National Park in the southwest corner of Utah when, quite by happenstance as it were, poor Nathan had been left behind. He had decided to mount an expedition into a nearby side canyon one morning and had become disoriented, wandering far from the main trail and spending the entire day sauntering at his ease midst the boulders and willows and deep pools that lay hidden back in amongst the narrow walls. He had been probing the mysteries of the place, oblivious to the passage of time when he finally realized that he had stayed much too long, for upon his return he discovered that the family had departed, had gone away and left him all alone.

He was disappointed, to be sure, a trifle miffed perhaps but nonetheless certain that he had not been spurned or callously cast aside. They Sanfords, however, were attorneys at law, people of obligations and affairs who were disinclined to waste much time on anything, much less rummaging through the wilderness for a wayward cat. But they were gone and would not return; of that he was also certain. And while Nathan was not exactly pleased with his situation, he understood the impatience of the human temperament and so more or less forgave them.

Nonetheless, they had ditched him and there he was, unattended, forlorn and very much aware of the fact that he needed to find his way back home as soon as possible. He had passed the night sleeping beneath the canopy of a large willow down by the river's edge, but he had not slept well. While the days were warm in this the season of the ebbing sun, the nights were not, were in fact cold as the heat of midday escaped rapidly into the dry desert air. That first night in the open canyon had been much colder than he could have ever imagined and he had slept but fitfully, shivering and squirming throughout. Certainly it was nothing like the ease to which he had become accustomed, nothing like the comfort of his bed back home in San Francisco, a Neiman Marcus bassinet replete with pillows and cotton blankets and a Raggedy Ann doll to keep him company.

He was dismayed, confused, fearful and hungry; but he was also conscious of the fact that neither Constance nor Harold nor Marisol nor anybody else was going to bring him food or solace or any other thing on that particular day. He was on his own and he knew it, realized at once that he would need to draw upon every resource at his command in order to survive, a daunting task for a cultivated cat like Nathan whose lone encounter with any kind of wilderness setting had been a brief sojourn long ago through the wilds of Golden Gate Park. He glanced briefly about, scanned the imposing monoliths of Zion that hovered high above, and was abashed. This cannot be happening to me, he said to himself, but of course it was and so he shook off the cold, sucked a deep breath and began to consider his options.

The sun by now had begun to clear the rim of the canyon as it rotated across the vast plateau high above, but down below in the depths of the great chasm the shadows would linger well into the day. It was silent, as always, in the early morning hours, dark and cool save for the gentle ripple of the Virgin River as it cut its way through the ancient tablelands. The course of the Virgin was brief and direct as it sliced downward across the Colorado Plateau, carving through the soft sandstone like a scalpel until it finally joined with the waters of the Colorado River, now trapped in a man made lake deep in the deserts of southern Nevada. The entire length of the Virgin was only several hundred miles, but during that span this diminutive river of the American southwest had sculpted one of the grand canyons of the world.

Awesome and noble was mighty Zion with its massive rock walls looming high above the river bed below, wondrous by whatever standard any sensitive feline cared to impose. There was, as well, a serenity that flowed through the canyon and permeated everywhere, an enduring tranquility, as if he had stumbled into some secret garden untrammeled since the dawning of time. He was truly captivated by the splendor and majesty of this great canyon, was very much tempted to linger awhile, to explore a bit further, but he knew he must make his way back to more hospitable surroundings without delay or he would be a very sad cat indeed, quickly surmising that his prospects for making a living down amongst the willow rushes and sand washes at the bottom of a deep canyon in southwest Utah were bleak at best.

And so he slowly began to make his way down along the banks of the Virgin. It was easy at first; he needed only to thread through the alders and assorted low shrubs that were spread out across the flood plain of the river. It was an open area down in this part of the canyon, flat and wide, and he made rapid progress. Near the entrance to the park the Virgin intersected several large campgrounds and as he sifted through the campsites he was treated to the full panoply of the human spectrum. How strange, Nathan thought to himself, to chance upon this motley and most curious collection of the human species right here in the heart of the Utah wilderness. Nonetheless, there they were and happy campers they seemed to be, all of them, in varied states of contentment.

There were affluent retirees tending to their well groomed motor homes, other less fortunate souls tucked away into their nylon tents, some folks in truck campers and a few wild and woolly types sleeping out in the open air wrapped only in their crusty blankets. It was at once a tapestry and embodiment of his cosmopolitan origins, a disparate assemblage of humanity that reminded him of his home back in San Francisco; but Zion Canyon was not Union Square and the landscape mainly caused him to lament the severity of his circumstance, prompted him to remember that he was a long way from Pacific Heights. And so he whimpered and mewed and shed tear or two, allowed himself a few seconds of self pity and then hurried on through as fast as he could.

He was at once forced to confront the solemn task that lay before him as the open valley soon gave way to more precipitous rock cliffs and dense undergrowth. It was difficult terrain and he was frequently obliged to travel along the shoulders of the local highway, moving quickly but cautiously as he tried to avoid the dust and debris churned up by the steady stream of onrushing cars. He sprinted through Springdale with its litany of motels and mini marts, on down through the valley of the Virgin, alternately contending against the hazards of nature and the perils of the open road. He was hungry but not starving since one kindly human in the campground, a jovial soul with ochre colored teeth and a big belly, had flipped him several slices of his half eaten breakfast bacon. It was not much and certainly not up to Nathan's usual standards, but it was enough for a cat and so he moved ahead, pushing relentlessly forward toward an ever expanding horizon.

Down through Hurricane and Washington and steadily onward until he finally reached interstate 15, ignoble, infamous I 15 which led on to St. George, Las Vegas and eventually into Los Angeles. Nathan himself knew nothing of interstate freeway systems or their numeric designations, but he did realize that this highway was another matter altogether, realized immediately that he had entered a more dangerous realm.

Huge trailer trucks, their eighteen wheels whining across the endless slabs of concrete, bore down on poor Nathan like great metal gargoyles, roaring past him as he scrambled along the shoulder, spewing out clouds of smoke in their wake as they rolled on towards whatever markets awaited them in Vegas and L.A. Nathan tried, whenever possible, to descend into the valley of the Virgin, but the going was slow down amongst the boulders and briar of the stream bed and so it was that he stayed mainly on the margins of the highway, struggling through the stench of gasoline and diesel fuel, through the blare and blast and clamor of hard charging interstate America, stepping lively along the fringe of unruly I 15, heading home, or so he hoped, to the city by the bay.

He skirted St. George, stronghold of the Latter Day Saints in southwestern Utah, even though it appeared to be a very clean and tidy place, righteous and chaste and altogether agreeable it seemed to him. Indeed, he was very much tempted to detour into that Mormon city with its alabaster temple rising up from the desert floor like some ancient fortress, was tempted to explore a bit further, but he knew he must not tarry. He gazed out across the desert lands that lay before him, unending they seemed now, undulating there in the shimmering white light of midday, and he knew he must keep moving.

In truth, he did not know precisely where he was at that very moment, not at all, but he had heard of a great, shining city that rose up from the empty deserts of southern Nevada, an unholy place, or so he had heard, of fast cats and easy money where all sense of daylight and darkness had melded into one great eternal glow of neon. It was a hellish place according to his informants, but it would at least offer some refuge for the night and so he quickly determined that must make Vegas before the setting of the sun.

Now Nathan could shake a tail when he had to, could move along at a very decent pace if the circumstances were sufficiently compelling, and that is exactly what he did. But it was exhausting. Scrambling down through the tangle and talus of the streambed, scraping his way back up to the menace of I 15—up and down, at times moving laterally across the slopes of the embankment, struggling mightily as he sought the safest and easiest route. Down through another deep gorge of the Virgin as it cut across a tiny slice of northwestern Arizona and then finally out into the remorseless heat of the vast Nevada desert. The way was flat and quick here however and he was able to gambol along at a steady pace. He did feel better now, less constrained by the vagaries of the canyonland terrain, and while he was hungry and tired he bounded easily across the open plain as he drew ever closer to the foreboding promise of Las Vegas.

Early twilight was just now beginning to settle across the desert, bathing the arid expanse in a lambent glow that hung like a curtain of lace above the untended wasteland and it was all quite lovely; but Nathan was too preoccupied to notice. I must make Vegas before nightfall, he kept saying to himself, or I am surely doomed and so he hastened his pace. He had abandoned the bed of the Virgin shortly after crossing into Nevada as the river swerved abruptly to the southwest on toward its union with Lake Mead and he was now heading on a westward course, following along the side of I 15 as it struck like an arrow straight for the heart of Vegas.

And it was easy—he was able to trot effortlessly through the rock scrabble of the treeless desert, avoiding all the greasy oil slicks and residue of burnt rubber that marred the surface of that remarkable thoroughfare. Onward he galloped, unyielding in his resolve, until finally, as the last vestige of twilight clung to the rim of the western horizon, he discerned the unmistakable glow of neon rising up from the desert floor and he knew he would at least survive another night.

He entered downtown as the last, faint rays of daylight were disappearing. The darkness would be absolute out there in the more remote reaches of the desert in this the beginning cycle of a new moon, but here in the crucible of downtown Las Vegas the transition was barely perceptible. Nathan knew San Francisco, had cruised Broadway during nighttime hours and had seen the bright lights of that city, but this was something beyond his experience. There were horseshoes and shamrocks, fantails and peacocks, all buzzing and hissing, tangled mazes of neon shimmering in the desert dusk, casting their sallow light across the glassy pavement.

It was at once garish and daunting, exciting yet vaguely sinister, a world apart that rose up from the desert floor like a beacon in an ocean of deep shadows. But such enticements to forbidden pleasures were lost on Nathan that evening; he was far too tired and so immediately began to seek some dark and tranquil alleyway where he could pass the night. But it was not easy, not in fabulous downtown Las Vegas.

Every corner, every crack and crevice, seemed to be illuminated; it was a city utterly aglow. Nathan, who regarded himself as a hep cat, a street wise, big city cat, was nonetheless astounded. It was a cauldron of light, all of it, an unrelenting flow of neon that tracked his every movement, a curse of incandescence and it was a nightmare for a tired and lonely, misplaced transient cat. Nevertheless, after several unsuccessful probes he finally wandered back into the dim reaches of one of the more secluded alleyways where he discovered some discarded cartons—ideal, he thought, for a peaceful night's sleep.

But as he slipped in behind one of the boxes, he inadvertently tripped over a large, pulsing hairy mass tucked away in silent repose into one of the corners. It was a snoozing rat and Nathan's sudden intrusion immediately caused him to awaken. The recalcitrant rodent rose up at once and began to threaten him, hissing and snarling and spewing saliva all over the place, an exceedingly unhappy rat who was fully prepared to defend his turf; and Nathan knew it.

This was, however, no ordinary rodent, not by any means. Nathan had encountered rats before, had done battle with them a number of times down in the Tenderloin in San Francisco, but this creature was a different species altogether. He was as big as a wombat it seemed—a sort of mutant rat spawned from the sordid entrails of that desert city, Nathan supposed—and he was as bellicose as he was large. He had risen up on his two hind legs and was growling now, eyes flaring, drool spilling from his darkly purpled lips, wheezing and snorting and fuming. A most serious kind of rat he was and he wasted no time, immediately lunging at Nathan and trying to snap a chunk out of his neck.

Nathan nearly fainted, nearly expired on the spot but managed instead to leap straight up and screech, more of a squeal of terror really which nonetheless managed to startle the rat and caused him to hesitate. Nathan took advantage of the brief lull, at once fleeing from the alley and back onto the main streets of the city. He was trembling now and still squealing as he sprinted away frantically, checking to his rear to see if the giant rat was following, which fortunately he was not. He thereupon sucked several deep breaths, silently admitted to himself that he had indeed embarked upon a dangerous trek and vowed to tread with considerably more caution in the future.

The constant glare of light notwithstanding, he soon discovered that the city was in fact a paradise for lost souls and vagrant cats, with nooks and niches and hidden corners everywhere and so he wasted no time in finding a ratless alcove behind some crates in one of the nearby alleyways. He was exhausted, drained to the core after the ordeal of his first day on the road and he immediately sank into a deep and most satisfying sleep. He awakened early the next morning just as the dim light of the approaching dawn began to filter through the haze of neon. He was a cool cat from a cool city and unaccustomed to warm climates, but he intuitively sensed that the heat would rise quickly out there in the low deserts of Nevada and so he once again began to prime himself for another long day.

The early morning hours in Vegas, while not exactly calm in any ordinary sense, were nonetheless more subdued than in the nighttime and he was able to move easily through the nearly empty streets. It was a strange and spectral scene that greeted him as he sifted through the maze of avenues and alleyways of downtown Las Vegas. The pale light of dawn mingled with the fading bloom from the casino marquees to create a kind of neon netherworld, an illusion of life force and energy that would somehow always fail to meet its promise, or so it seemed to Nathan as he slipped into one of his more contemplative moods. And while he was tempted to explore a bit further, he felt curiously uneasy and so hurried through the center of town as fast as he could.

His instincts continued to pull him on a north westerly bearing; it was uncanny and strange, but he innately sensed that he was always going in the right direction, was confident that he would sooner or later arrive safely back home in San Francisco, knew it in his heart and never wavered for a second as he continued to push ahead, weaving up through the unsavory array of trailer parks and housing tracts of North Las Vegas, onward toward the city limits where he finally burst into the open desert once again.

He had been hungry upon awakening, but he soon discovered that feeding oneself was an easy chore in the gambling towns of Nevada. During the day and all through the night the casinos dumped tons of uneaten, half digested food into their garbage heaps and while these great pyres of edible refuse were aesthetically displeasing, at least to a cat like Nathan, they were abundant and easily accessible. He had, therefore, been able to gorge himself, cramming food into his gullet until he was sated and while he would be dyspeptic and farting like a steam locomotive for several days to come, he was nonetheless relatively well nourished as he located Highway 95 and crossed over into the hardscrabble deserts of western Nevada.

He was moving steadily now as he bounded along the arid fringes that bordered route 95. This road, however, was nothing like the terror of I 15, was in fact nearly deserted. It was obvious to him that he was rapidly drawing away from the sprawl of human settlement down in Vegas and into a separate domain. And although he could move with ease through the vacant terrain, loping along smoothly to the rhythm of his natural gait, the rising heat and unremitting monotony of the desert began to weigh on him.

The constancy of the landscape here was relentless, remained unbroken mile after mile, crest after barren crest, valley after barren valley, an incessant staccato of sagebrush and greasewood in never ending procession. The sense of isolation was nearly absolute out there in the Great Basin of Nevada and for the first time since his departure from Zion he began to wonder about his prospects. Nonetheless, he struggled forward, pushed valiantly ahead into the ominous blaze of an ascending sun, for it was all that he could really do, all that he really knew how to do.

Onward and onward he galloped, plunging ever further into the empty expanse of the Nevada desert, scampering across the parched earth and stone rubble until at last he knew he must rest awhile. It was just then that he spotted a small cluster of shrub willows flanking a lone Palo Verde tree off into the distance, mirage like it was, shimmering there in the surging heat of midday. And while it was far to the east of his intended course and would represent a deviation of at least a half an hour or more, he did not hesitate; he was exhausted and dehydrated, half baked to the bone and needed a few moments respite.

Upon arriving, he at once realized that he had been blessed as he beheld the miniature oasis—not only did it provide a refuge from the heat, but there was a small trickle of water that seeped up to the surface from some hidden spring, life sustaining water, cool and clear, and he silently rejoiced. He immediately began to fill himself, drank blissfully until he could drink no more, and then fell asleep beneath the branches of the stalwart Palo Verde.

Upon awakening he realized that something was wrong, sensed at once that there was an alien presence in the air. He heard it at first, a hollow, buzzing sound that was akin to the whirr of a grasshopper, but much louder and much more penetrating. And then he saw it, not two feet from where he lay, a large diamondback rattlesnake wound into a tight spiral, tongue flicking in out, poised to strike at the slightest provocation. It was an evil looking creature, thick and heavy, its triangular head bobbing from side to side with lifeless eyes staring out blankly toward Nathan.

The snake had come to the tiny oasis in order to drink from the spring and had only by chance discovered a sleeping cat. But the rattlesnake's vision was poor; it relied instead upon heat sensors imbedded in its constantly probing tongue, a tongue that was both sensitive and accurate and he could easily tell that this creature lying there in front of him was considerably larger than the rats and other rodents that he normally fed upon, could tell by the amount of heat being generated by this pudgy little ball of fur that this was no ordinary morsel. And so it hesitated.

Nathan, however, knew nothing of the rattlesnake's calculations; he only knew that this reptilian interloper was causing him a serious problem. He was, of course, ignorant of his own mortality, knew nothing of death as an inevitable termination of his existence, but he did know that the snake could kill him, understood that his life lay in the balance at that very moment, that his very survival depended on the whims of this cold-blooded, primordial creature that swayed ominously not two feet from his face.

He was ill informed of snakes in general, nothing of their habits or temperaments, nothing of their predilections—there were no snakes in his neighborhood in Pacific Heights—but he intuitively sensed that this reptile looming up in front of him, weaving and bobbing, tongue flicking in and out, was not much inclined toward introspection, was in fact most likely programmed to act on instinct alone. And so Nathan had to decide what to do, had to try and divine the inherent propensities of this creature whose evolutionary development had concluded several million years ago.

Essentially he had two choices—he could make a dash for it, leap suddenly forward and try to evade the serpent's strike, or he could wait it out and hope that the rattlesnake would simply go away. The first option did not seem encouraging—we cats have been around for awhile as well, he said to himself, and do understand that these reptiles have not survived for as long as they have by being slow to the kill. And so he decided to do nothing, to lie there as still as possible and pray that the snake would just slither away.

But it was not easy. Every fiber and sinew in his body screamed out to flee; it was an inborn impulse, was in fact, along with scratching, the primary means of self-defense for all domesticated felines everywhere. But he stayed where he was, fought every instinct in his being and remained motionless, barely breathing in that eerie suspension of time as the snake swayed back and forth, hooded eyes fixed straight ahead. He waited for what seemed to be several lifetimes, patiently abiding, until finally the rattlesnake dipped back down, slid gracefully from its coil and glided back out into the desert.

Nathan wasted not an instant contemplating his good fortune, tarried not at all, rather exploded from beneath the shelter of the Palo Verde and vaulted out into the open desert like a cat possessed. He had been terror stricken for those few minutes while the snake hovered there in front of him, had been absolutely certain that he was doomed. But he had been spared and now was numb to everything save the peremptory fact of his own survival. The heat was inexorable at this hour of the day as the sun rotated ever higher into the cloudless sky smothering everything in its path, but Nathan little noted nor scarcely heeded the discomfort of it all. He knew only that he was alive and so he bounded across the sun baked desert floor with utter abandon, sailed across the empty wastelands like a zephyr, mindless of anything but the fact of his continued existence.

He kept heading northward until he reached the junction at highway 6 and then, quite suddenly and with no logical inducement to do so, swerved west on into the state of California. It was a primal response, a mandate from the deeper reaches of his instincts and it was impelling. And so he veered sharply right and continued pushing onward as the sun slid further toward the distant horizon, its angle more oblique now, less punishing than before. He was still in a desert, no doubt, but the landscape had begun to slowly change, was slightly more benign here, a kinder and gentler place as the hardscrabble pan of the Nevada basin began to yield to erratic clusters of alder and willow groves. And in the distance he began to perceive, vaguely limned through the haze of the lingering heat, the outline of a significant mountain range.

It was the Sierra Nevada, fabled Range of Light, and Nathan suddenly realized that he was not that far from home. He remembered, indistinctly but with certainty, that the family had crossed a major mountain range shortly after leaving their home in San Francisco and he apprehended at once that this must be it. And so he accelerated his pace, exhausted though he was, as the expectation of arriving safely back home to the sweet embrace of his beloved family caused a massive explosion of adrenaline to surge through his weary body.

Onward and onward he galloped, pushing forward, using the rise and dip of the ridgeline as his guide, pressing relentlessly ahead, closing the distance between him and his cozy little bassinet back home in Pacific Heights. He eventually joined with highway 395 where he swung immediately to the north. He was seeking a route through the lofty Sierra Nevada now, only that and nothing more, and once again his instincts advised him that this route 395 was destined to lead him home. Onward he sped, passing by June Lake and up toward Lee Vining—if only I can cross these mountains he said to himself, if only I can reach the other side I will certainly make it back home to San Francisco.

The sun by now had dipped below the crest line and the air had turned suddenly cooler. The general aspect of the landscape was gradually beginning to shift as the sparse vegetation of the lower deserts began to give way to large stands of Pine and Spruce. Nathan, being the cat that he was, knew nothing of geographic transitions of course, but he did realize that he had been moving steadily upward ever since he had crossed over into California, higher and higher, until he had finally penetrated into the sub alpine zones of the eastern Sierra. And while the coolness was a blessing, to be sure, the air here in the mountains was much thinner, contained less oxygen, and it was only with the greatest of difficulty that he was able to maintain any kind of reasonable pace.

His breathing was more labored now and his tiny heart seemed ready to explode at any moment; nonetheless he continued struggling onward and upward, even as twilight began to fade, pressing forward until he eventually joined with route 120, which cut abruptly to the west. He paused a few seconds, but his instincts once again informed him that this was surely the way home and so he hung a left turn and scurried forward. The road here became much steeper however, much more arduous and difficult, but Nathan nevertheless continued to push ahead, wheezing and gasping, desperate to cross the mountains before the setting of the sun. But the darkness was everywhere by then and so when he finally stumbled out into a large, open meadow, he immediately scrambled over to the protection of a large Ponderosa Pine beneath which he instantly collapsed into a deep and soundless sleep.

When he awakened the next morning, he again sensed that something was amiss, could feel in his feline bones that he wasn't alone anymore. He slowly and apprehensively raised his eyes upward, fully anticipating the worst, lifting his gaze skyward until he finally beheld the hulking mass of a huge California Brown Bear hovering there directly above him, not three feet from where he lay.

They both stared at each other for a long while, too long it seemed to Nathan, neither one stirring nor making a sound as the amber light of the mountain dawn began to glisten off the nearby granite cliffs. Unlike the rat and rattlesnake, however, this bear simply seemed to be satisfying his curiosity, paying his respects as it were, and aside from the compelling fact of his presence suggested nothing in the way of a menace or threat. Nonetheless, poor Nathan little trusted nor much liked these wilderness creatures and was singularly disinterested in initiating any kind of social or psychic intercourse; was, in fact, properly terrified.

But the bear, who had probably been nourishing himself on a steady diet of garbage for the past ten years or so, simply passed a thunderous amount of gas and then quietly wandered off, unperturbed and indifferent. As both a consequence of nerves and intestinal discomfort, Nathan passed a bit of gas himself, vowing as he did so to never again eat any more garbage once he got back home to San Francisco and vowing as well to never again take another trip with Constance and Harold; then he turned and judiciously began to consider his circumstance.

He was at the base of the east entrance into Yosemite National Park in the heart of another vast wilderness preserve in the great American West. It was cold here and the frost flecked air sparkled in the soft light of the dawning day. There was a loveliness to the place that was mystical and he was tempted to linger for awhile, was tempted in fact to stay there forever, but he knew he must get moving, was by now thoroughly disinclined to commit his fate to the vagaries of the natural universe. He glanced skyward, briefly contemplating the massive rock walls that girded the western edge of the meadowlands, then drew a deep breath and promptly proceeded to move upward across the stately Sierras on toward his home back in San Francisco.

The road ascended abruptly at first as it traversed the huge rock face of the eastern scarp, switching back and forth as it rose ever higher. But Nathan was well rested now and his spirit was singing as he glided easily upward toward the pass. He was certain that he recognized the place, remembered it from the trip over with his family, and so was buoyant and confident as he made his way toward the higher elevations. There was very little traffic on the road in the early morning hours and he was able to move freely across the cool surface of the highway. He passed by the unmanned entrance station and continued on up until he finally cleared into the broad expanse of the Tuolomne Meadows, glowing softly now in the pale light of the Sierra sunrise.

It was enchanting up here in this high mountain meadow, a nearly perfect place cloistered in snow capped mountain peaks and gleaming rock, lush and verdant and peaceful and again he was tempted to linger for awhile; but he did not. Rather he kept pushing ahead, loping along now to his heart's delight as the terrain became more genial and more forgiving. He was crossing over Tioga Pass, a natural breech in the mountains that was gently rolling and temperate and so he was able to move quickly and easily. The sun was rotating higher and higher into the eastern sky by now and the full light of mid morning sparkled off the silent waters of the nearby lakes and tarns, glistened everywhere off the golden meadows, as Nathan, exultant and joyous in the anticipation of the comforts to which he had become accustomed, headed back to his home in Pacific Heights.

Across the pass, galloping now, downward he plunged through the dense forests of the western slope, bounding along the side of highway 120 as it looped its sinuous path down through the Sierra foothills, desperately wishing to reach San Francisco by nightfall. On past Oakdale and finally out into the great central valley of California where he recognized it all, remembered well the small towns, the infinite swath of orchard and vegetable farms, the grand sweep of cropland that flourished here in the fertile soils of western California. It was all quite inelegant, he mused, redundant and tedious it seemed to him, especially after the recent splendor of the high Sierra; nonetheless, it was the cornucopia of America, the fruit and vegetable basket of half a continent and was imposing in its way, he supposed.

But he was indifferent to it all really, anxious only to once again be cruising the streets of his native San Francisco. Nonetheless, it was not easy—there was more congestion down lower in the valley, much more, as the urban fragrance of gasoline fume and steaming tar rose up to mingle with the swirling dust of the dry valley floor. Nathan was necessarily forced over onto the periphery and down into the gullies along side the shoulder of the highway where he had to contend with all the debris and assorted litter of a modern, mobile America.

His pace slowed considerably then, diminished to a trot in fact as he finally came to realize that he would never arrive in San Francisco that night. After a brief search, he soon discovered a small pocket scooped from the muck of a concrete culvert close to the city of Manteca where he packed himself in for the evening, slipping easily into a satisfying sleep as visions of his home in San Francisco wound pleasantly through his dreams.

Once again he awakened early, but here in the scruffy central valley of California the clarity of the mountain air had been purged, had been replaced by a dull, ashen haze that hung over the broad expanse like a damp blanket. The heat down here was oppressive, had never really abated during the night and as Nathan stretched himself into wakefulness he once again considered his circumstance, carefully weighed all the aspects of his situation and gradually concluded that this last segment of the long journey could well be the most perilous of all. For he did know the area, had traveled through Manteca before with his family and was painfully conscious of the fact that from here on into San Francisco the route would be a vortex of rampaging steel.

Indeed, automobiles and trucks and everything else that rolled would be gushing out of the foothills from every direction and funneling into interurban route 580, ominous 580, the main artery into San Francisco from this region. Motorized vehicles of every ilk and brand, every shape and color, from 18-wheelers to motorcycles, from Volkswagens to XKEs, all came careening down 580 heading for the bay. And Nathan knew for a fact, knew it like an imprint on his heart, that a tiny little cat like himself would be squashed like a bug beneath that ponderous crush of metal, wouldn't have chance; so as he slowly shook off the drowsiness of early morning and commenced to clean himself, he abruptly but firmly decided that he must hitch a ride into the city.

Now a hitchhiking cat would be an absurdity and Nathan knew it, had no intention in fact of sticking out his paw for the purpose of soliciting a ride. No way. For Nathan was a hip cat, clued in to the ways of the world and he knew it would be an easy task to hop up onto the open bed of any one of the many trucks that were always parked in front of Calhoun's Auto Oasis near the outskirts of Manteca. The trucks would be vacant while the drivers were inside resting and feeding themselves, regaling each other with tales of the open road, and it would be an uncomplicated matter to jump up onto any one of them. The problem was to select a truck whose destination would be San Francisco rather than Oakland or San Jose or some other strange and alien outpost, and he could really do no more than make a random choice, eliminate the ones loaded with goat manure and other diverse agricultural products perhaps, but in the end he would be forced to submit to the vagaries of chance.

And so he leapt up into a late model, full ton Ford pick up with California plates laden with a clutter of antique furniture and other assorted collectibles—a San Francisco cargo if he ever saw one, he surmised—where he proceeded to curl up into a darkened corner and quickly doze off. He had no idea how long he had slept when he was abruptly awakened by the roar of the engine as the truck lurched forward and rolled out toward turbulent 580. Nathan never did see the driver of the vehicle, never would see the man, but it was of no matter to him really. He knew only that he had embarked on the final leg of a long and wearisome journey, one that had begun in the valley of the Virgin River in Zion National Park in the state of Utah and was about to draw to a close.

Nathan immediately scrambled up onto a nearby chair so that he could see what was happening. His heart was heaving now and his mind was spinning wildly as he settled down into its deep cushions in order to monitor the final passage on into the city. Or so he hoped—he also needed to insure that this driver did not suddenly exit unto some wayward route, was not headed into some anonymous suburban hinterland where poor Nathan could wander around for years trying to find his way out. He was too close to home now for any meaningless detours and knew that he must be prepared to bail out at any instant. But he was blessed this day, or so it seemed, as they continued to roll onward down through Tracy and Livermore, across the arid coastal hills past Castro Valley and on into Oakland.

With every passing mile feral 580 swelled with the congestion of urban cartage, but Nathan the Cat was unperturbed by any of it. He was securely installed in the richly embroidered cushions of the comfortable antique chair and felt very much at home. As they approached the Bay Bridge he strained to snatch a glimpse of the great Pyramid of Trans America that rose up in capitalistic grandeur from the center of San Francisco. When he first caught sight of it, he broke into a sweat and as they drew ever closer to the toll booths his eyeballs began to stream and his throat went dry and when the truck paused to pay the fee he completely lost it, urinated involuntarily onto that priceless antique chair and nearly tumbled from the truck in a seismic fit of ecstasy.

They continued across and exited immediately onto the Embarcadero. Nathan was nearly beside himself by now and when the driver rolled to a stop at the Market Street intersection, he decided to take his leave. He knew exactly where he was at this juncture and was ill disposed to take any more chances and so hopped out, unnoticed by the driver, and headed up Market. He breathed deeply of the salt flavored air as he sailed along San Francisco's main boulevard, savoring the taste and texture of it all. He knew his way home from here and so his pace quickened as he cruised through the heart of the city. On up Market and through the Tenderloin where he offered a brief greeting to some of the alley cats whom he had befriended over the years, then over to Larkin and up to Pacific, the street on which he lived.

He was bounding now, exuberant with anticipation as he crossed Van Ness and raced onward, indifferent to the steep hills, insensible to everything about him, conscious only of the fact that he would soon be home. Was focused on that and nothing more. For he had indeed prevailed, had survived the scree and bramble of the canyons, the heat and monotony of the deserts, the terror of the interstates, mutated rats, ominous reptiles and flatulent bears. Had endured all of it and now was within a few blocks of home, could in fact discern in the distance the familiar outline of the beloved manse in which he resided.

And then, just as he wheeled abruptly right to cross Pacific, he suddenly heard the shrill squeal of automobile tires and vaguely glimpsed the flash of chrome as the vehicle loomed up in front of him. No, no, no he said to himself screaming silently into the horror of it all, this cannot be happening. Cannot. Cannot. And then quite curiously, or so he thought to himself in that ultimate, chilling instant, he heard the squish of his own body being flattened out onto the faded urban pavement as the car sped away on toward other unknown destinations, either unaware or unconcerned with the incident at hand.

The fog was lifting now and the shallow sunlight of early morning had begun to seep through the lingering haze as the denizens of Pacific Heights surfaced from their doorways and scurried off toward their daily chores. Several minutes later Harold and Phoebe and Marisol emerged from their tidy Victorian manor and made their way up Pacific on over to Van Ness where they would hail a taxi and head off to their respective assignments for the day. They had by now adjusted to Nathan's absence, had in fact begun a new search for his replacement. They didn't notice the smear of blood pulp in the middle of the street, were heedless to the tufts of gray fur floating up through the morning air, absorbed as they were in their own private reveries, moving mindlessly through a world far removed from the canyons of Utah and desert lands of Nevada, unaware, it would seem, that Nathan the Cat had finally made it home.

BEATRICE THE GUANACO

It would be a long passage. Long and difficult. One full cycle of the sun had come and gone since she first spotted the lone condor drifting silently back and forth across the high plateau. It circled gracefully, soaring and dipping in concert with the swirling currents of mountain air, wasting little energy in the process. And she knew it was tracking her, knew it sensed her desperation and was but patiently abiding.

As well, the chill of early morning was lingering now into late afternoon, a deep, penetrating cold that dulled her sense and slowed her pace. She was anxious in the contemplation of what lay ahead, the fierce storms that could come roaring through the Andean highlands with no warning, the specter of being isolated and all alone in an unknown mountain wilderness. But more compelling by far was the presence of the condor, for she knew that there was a purpose to the tenacity of the large bird and she feared for her life.

She had been foraging with her family, grazing near the shores of Lake Titicaca when she had been implausibly snatched away one dark and moonless night. It had happened during a violent storm, a sudden explosion that had come roaring down the surrounding mountainsides and cast her to the wind, sweeping her away to distant parts. So she was searching for her family now, anxiously combing the barren slopes, calling out into the vast Andean void. And it was baneful for her, the enduring cold, the loneliness, the immensity of the place, all of it an affliction beyond anything she could have ever imagined, rendered ever more ominous by the unremitting shadow of the condor as it glided back and forth across the mountainsides stalking her every movement.

Her prospects were not encouraging. Beatrice made her home on the Bolivian Altiplano, a high basin in the Andes Mountains that was 500 miles long and nearly 80 miles wide, a vast plateau that sloped gently to the south at elevations between 11,000 and 13,000 feet. It was an austere and barren land, cold and raw, a great inter montane valley formed by the separation of two distinct mountain ridges, the Cordilleras Oriental and Occidental. Near the city of La Paz to the north the Oriental was known as the Real and contained a string of snow bound mountain peaks that ran for more than 200 miles at an average height of nearly 18,000 feet.

The northern terminus of the altiplano lay in the shadow of these great summits and it was here, high up on the windblown crests of the cordillera, that Beatrice had been stranded. It was a majestic setting, a treeless, rock-strewn stretch of arid mountain land that gleamed like a string of pearls in the clarity of the Andean skies; but it was, as well, a fierce and foreboding place, an austere landscape hostile to habitation of any kind and Beatrice knew that if she did not soon find her family, or at the very least some source of nourishment, she would surely perish.

The power of the big storm had been fearsome, had been a horror for her, a holocaust of wind that had arrived like some evil spirit spiraling down from the mountaintops. The family had retired for the evening to a small meadow of bunchgrass near Titicaca, Beatrice, her mother, four brothers and Eddie the dominant male, all of them in peaceful repose after a long day of grazing. It was during the cycle of a new moon and the darkness had been nearly absolute, deeper than ebony that night with only a few scattered stars glimmering faintly in the distance, an indistinct glow that burned but dimly in the vast expanse of cosmos.

She remembered only the great roar that immediately preceded the arrival of the storm, a sudden peal of thunder that seemed to have rolled in from some alien latitude, as if the heavens themselves had burst apart. She had been abruptly wrenched from the bed of alders where she was sleeping and from that point forward everything had become a blur in the convulsion of the ensuing maelstrom.

There was no chance to do anything as the massive surge of down sloping air lifted her from where she lay and scooped her away, skimming and bouncing across the darksome plain as if she were a piece of dry straw. The force of the wind was beyond anything she had ever experienced before, remorselessly driving her across the high plateau, careening helplessly over the hard surface of the valley floor, crashing blindly through the darkness. It had been a tumult of chaos and confusion during which time she had closed her eyes and tried to relax as best she could; but it had been impossible and she could do little more than accede to the power of the big storm.

Now and again she would manage to struggle to her feet, would attempt to regain her equilibrium, but it was useless. The strength of the wind was transcendent as it tore across the open expanse, stripping everything in its path, small shrubs and shards of loose rock everywhere flying through the air as Beatrice flailed and thrashed away with her hooves, writhing and twisting against the demonic winds, squealing helplessly into the void until at last she realized that she could really do nothing more than passively abide.

She had become addled in the course of events, oblivious to the passage of time, but when at last the storm weakened and died she noted that the thin crescent of a new moon had arced far into the western sky and so she knew it had lasted for awhile. As the turbulence subsided an eerie calm began to settle across the land, but it was still dark and she was unable to see anything, unable to orient herself to the new surroundings. Nonetheless, she could tell that she had been carried far away and deposited in a different place, could feel it in the coldness of the mountain air and hear it in the silence of the stars; could sense it everywhere all about her.

She knew she had been badly mauled, battered and cleft from shoulder to shank, could feel the pain coursing everywhere throughout her young and fragile body. She immediately wondered if she had been seriously hurt, worried that she may have been somehow mortally wounded, but knew as well that she would have to wait until first light before she could determine the extent of the injuries; and so she drew herself up into a ball and tried to sleep, but sleep did not come easily and she could do nothing more than restively wait the coming dawn.

That first day broke clear and cold as the thin light of early morning rose up from the distant ridgelines and slowly filled the sky. She awakened at once and stretched herself back into consciousness, slowly checking for the presence of any grievous injury and while she ached terribly through all her parts and the gashes and cuts were everywhere throbbing with pain, her limbs and vital organs all seemed to be free from serious damage.

There were no pools of blood anywhere that she could see, no steady flow of fluids from any part of her and so she cautiously rose to her feet and tried to walk. It was tenuous at first as she tottered and swayed midst the violent gusts of wind that forever raked the Andean highlands, desperately struggling to maintain her balance. She was, however, able to move forward without falling, weaving and stumbling to be sure, but nonetheless able to cope; and while it was both vexing and painful, the injuries seemed to be neither mortal nor disabling and so she finally settled back on her rear haunch and carefully began to consider her circumstance.

She had been dropped onto the northern flank of Illimani, one of the several peaks that soared high above the valley floor at the northern tip of the altiplano, far from any place she had ever known before. The terrain here was much steeper than the gently sloping alluvial fans of the lower plateau where she normally roamed, steeper and ever more desolate. The topsoil had long ago been stripped away by wind and melting snow and while it was all pristine and radiant in the thin air of the mountain dawn, it was for Beatrice a strange and alien land. No storm could be so powerful to have carried me this far, she said to herself, no wind so strong. But there she was, stranded high upon the narrow northern ridge of mighty Illimani amongst the scree and boulders and howling wind, forlorn and bereft of hope.

Lake Titicaca lay in the distance far below, shimmering brightly in the wake of an ascending sun and she immediately sensed that she must somehow reach that lake if she were to survive. There was nothing to eat up there on the barren slopes of that mountain side, nothing at all and she knew that she must somehow gain the fertile strandline that girded Titicaca or else she would die. Beatrice had no idea where her mother and sisters and Eddie the male might be, knew not even if they were still alive; she knew only that she must strike for the big lake down below, must gain its verdant shores or surely perish.

But she had been wandering now for three days and was growing very weak and very weary. The lake, for certain, had seemed far away when she began, but not unreachable; nonetheless, as she continued to move forward the distance seemed never to close, seemed always to remain constant. She would from time to time stray off toward an adjacent valley or would climb to the crest of a small rise in order to search for her family, but there was never any trace of anyone; nothing but the shifting of the winds as they swept across the empty mountainsides—nothing but the endless expanse of cloudless sky and broken rock.

And it was discouraging for her, all of it; nonetheless, she never abandoned hope, not for an instant, for she knew that if they were still alive they would never forswear their search, would never relent in their efforts to find her. Knew it like an imprint on her heart and drew strength from that knowledge. Mainly, however, she continued to bore directly for the great lake, steadily and with decision, persistently forging ahead, but it seemed never to draw closer, remained elusive and chimerical out in the distance, glimmering silently in the frigid air of the high plateau.

And always the shadow of the huge condor hovered above her, sweeping back and forth like a curse, was her constant companion as it patiently tracked her movements through the long days. She would try to sleep during the hours of darkness, would seek some small alcove or bunker cut back into the slope of the mountainside. But it was difficult. The cold penetrated everywhere at the high elevations, drove down bone deep and caused her to tremble and moan all through the night. She would sleep awhile and then suddenly awaken, chattering and shivering, would then shift positions and try to fall asleep again. And so it would continue, endless cycles of restless sleep and anguished wakefulness, always cold, always trembling.

Through the daylight hours she would advance steadily forward and downward, moving tentatively now as her strength began to wane, nonetheless continuing dauntlessly on toward the lake. She was growing weaker with each passing hour however, had eaten nothing in fact for three days now and so would occasionally stumble and fall as her hooves became tangled in the drifts of rubble that were scattered randomly across the hillsides. And it was a torment for her, astray in an empty place of shattered rock and little else, a land pounded by eons of wind and snow and rain, cold and forbidding, a wild, desolate land consigned to the fringes of time.

Then one morning she slipped and fell into a ravine. It was a careless error, one born of deep fatigue and it was a grave misfortune. She had been traversing a thin ridgeline that divided two steep canyons when her left, front hoof skimmed off a boulder that was half buried in the shadows of a larger rock. A thin glaze of ice, imperceptible, had formed across the surface of the boulder and caught her by surprise.

She was a surefooted creature, as were all guanacos, deft and agile amongst the scrub and gravel of the altiplano and she would have regained her balance under normal circumstances. But not this time—she was too weary and too weak. She had plunged head long down the nearly vertical slope, tumbling and crashing, spiraling forward, bouncing off the boulders and bushes and scree of the frozen mountainside until she finally came to rest in the bough of an alder shrub down in the darkened folds of some anonymous canyon on the western flank of Illimani.

It was the worst of circumstances and she knew it. She lay there on her back cradled by the branches of the stunted alder wondering then if she were still alive, staring into an indistinct firmament as earth and heaven melded together overhead into a milky haze, all of it spinning wildly above her. She became suddenly nauseous and her stomach began to convulse, but there was nothing to purge. She had not eaten for three days now and so she could do nothing more than retch in a violent series of dry contractions, gasping and choking, tears streaming from her eyes as she strived to gain command of her senses.

And it was an agony for her; she was cold and lonely and sealed off from everything she had ever known— forlorn and desperate beyond her capacity to even comprehend. Worse yet, a slow pain had begun to thrum up from the base of her left flank, barely perceptible at first but quite real and she knew she had been injured. It was a dull pain, distant and muted, but it was there and she was instinctively aware that her body had been damaged; knew it for a fact and despaired at the thought.

Beatrice, of course, was unaware of her own mortality, knew nothing of the inevitability of death as a natural consequence of her existence, but she did understand that her very life wavered on the edge down there in the dim recesses of that canyon, depended in fact upon her resolve and willingness to respond; and she had no intention of yielding gracefully.

But it was not easy. She wept for a short while, silently and shamelessly, then reluctantly began to gird herself for the struggle that lay ahead. The climb up from the bottom of the canyon would be onerous and she feared for her chances, instinctively knew that she was far too weak to gain the upper reaches of the canyon. But even worse perhaps was the threat of the condor as she once again glimpsed the shadow of the great bird, menacing as it swung back and forth across the open breach of the ravine and she could tell he had tightened his orbit, could see that he was beginning to drop down lower—and she knew he had begun his earthward descent.

As she lay there trembling, struggling to regain some composure and perspective, her thoughts drifted back to an earlier time, another time several years ago when her life had also swung in the balance. It was further south in the mountains that flanked the eastern edge of the Atacama Desert in the north of Chile. It had been during the winter season when the arc of the sun was at its lowest ebb, the season of deep cold when the icy winds of Patagonia roared up from Anarctica and ravaged the high deserts of the southern sphere, the darkest time of the year when she had suddenly fallen ill. She had lain there feverish and shivering, tucked into a small thicket of scrub alder beneath a rock outcropping as her auntie Alice tended to her needs. The other members of the clan had been roaming the hillsides foraging for food at the time and so as yet were unaware of the gravity of her circumstance.

It was dangerous terrain to have been grazing in the first place, hunting grounds of the Puma, big cat of the Americas, powerful and cunning predator of the Andes. But they had been very hungry, all of them, undernourished and desperate and the feeding could be good on the lower slopes of the eastern cordillera; and so they had decided to risk it. But Beatrice had taken sick, was languishing there in the shadows of the rock scarp as the fever rapidly spread through her weakened body.

She had begun to wail and moan, unconsciously and unwillingly, even though she knew that her lamentations would carry far into the cold, dry air of the Atacama, would echo out across the open mountainsides and inevitably attract the Puma. Her auntie tried to console her, tried to soothe her discomfort as best she could, but it was futile as Beatrice continued to wail all through the day and into the night; and they both knew that sooner or later the Puma, always on the prowl in this his natural habitat, would surely hear her cries.

The cat appeared suddenly, sprang up from the shadows and landed softly on the ledge of an adjacent boulder. It was a large male and he was growling low, a portentous, malevolent purr as he crouched down on his rear haunch, hovering there nervously, poised to pounce. His teeth gleamed like polished ivory in the Andean twilight and his eyes glowed yellow as he slouched there in tense anticipation of the kill. He was a mature cat, thick through the shoulders with a snow-white belly and dark tinged ear tips. The whole of his torso rippled with strength as he hunkered there, slunk down low, ready to leap out at the slightest provocation; but he hesitated.

He was surprised, no doubt, to have chanced upon two hopelessly vulnerable guanacos; one alone would provide a complete meal, but two of them huddled helplessly in front of him posed a problem and he knew not precisely what to do. Powerful and quick though he was, he could in no way manage to subdue two adult guanacos in one sudden strike and he was momentarily confused.

By now Beatrice was bleating wildly into the rising wind, thoroughly terrified, bawling and puling. The

Puma was glancing nervously back and forth from one to the other, teeth bared, softly growling, squatting down low on his hind shank, massive shoulders tensed and trembling. Beatrice had been certain she was doomed when quite suddenly and without warning her auntie, who had remained calm throughout, leapt up and bolted from the thicket.

The big cat was on the fleeing guanaco at once, snatched her by the throat and slammed her to the ground where he commenced to tighten his hold and slowly strangle her to death. Beatrice, weak and quavering beyond control by now, nonetheless managed to crawl out from under the alcove and bury herself beneath a nearby pile of rotting tree limbs. She watched helplessly, softly moaning through it all as her valiant but defenseless aunt flailed and thrashed about, kicking and squalling, then finally falling into silence; and Beatrice could do nothing more than lie there, observing in soundless horror as the hungry Puma tore into her auntie Alice.

The cat wasted little time in consuming the carcass, stripped the flesh and devoured everything within a few hours save for the hair and bones as Beatrice silently looked on, huddled in the shadows, watching mournfully as the Puma engorged himself. He finally departed after having sated his hunger, unmindful of Beatrice's presence, wandering off in search of future prey. When her family returned she was close to death, shivering silently in the darkness of the alder branches, too weak to even cry. Her mother had nursed her back to health that season, carefully and with infinite patience, until Beatrice had finally regained most of her strength; but the healing had been incomplete, a grueling and tedious passage from which she had never fully recovered.

Nonetheless, she had survived and in the remembrance of it she realized that her auntie had fled the thicket on purpose, had sacrificed herself in order that Beatrice might live. And while the recollection of that mortal encounter would forever cause her to grieve, it had also caused her to understand that she could always rely upon the family to nurture and protect her. She often wept at the thought of the passing of her aunt, wailed far into the night at times and it saddened her even now; but she was also aware that all of that was in the past, had nothing to do with her present circumstance and so she quickly abandoned the memory and began to measure her possibilities.

First of all she knew she needed to assess the severity of her injuries, for she could tell that something had been seriously damaged. The pain by now had begun to focus and deepen, was much more intense and she immediately suspected that she had cracked some ribs; maybe more, but for certain the ribs on her left flank were either split or broken. She tried to regain her feet and after several stumbling attempts was able to do so, but with every movement, every flex and twitch, the pain cut deeper, sliced like a scalpel through her rib cage and caused tears to come to her eyes.

Nonetheless, she was able to move, very slowly and at a mere hobble, but sufficient to let her inch her way out of the tangle of scrub alder and out into the more open areas of the canyon floor. But it was difficult down there in the entrails of that sunless ravine, no more than a slit really in the vast expanse of the Andean highlands, and she began to wonder if it were going to be worth the effort.

And always, without surcease, the shadow of the condor flicked back and forth at the edge of her vision, hovering on the rim, circling ever lower, moving downward in ever tightening spirals. Beatrice was aware that these great birds were eaters of carrion, fed solely on the residue of the already dead and rotting, but there was something different about this one, something vaguely sinister. Back and forth it came, swinging lower and lower, descending steadily now and she knew that it was planning to kill her.

Beatrice sensed that her only option was to seek an open space up along the slopes of the canyon wall where some member of her family might possibly spot her. She knew that they would be searching, endlessly combing the mountainsides in an effort to find her, was certain of it and so understood that she must somehow reach a place where she could be seen. It was in fact all that she could really do for she had neither the energy nor the strength to attain the ridgeline high above; it was a dire and deadly circumstance, no doubt, but if she could reach the narrow shelf above she might have a chance.

She was surrounded by steep cliffs strewn with endless tracts of scree and it would be a travail, a labor of mortal consequence. Nonetheless, her only other option was to lie down and slowly yield to the darkness, seek a comfortable place among the alders and allow herself to pass in peaceful repose. But if I must die, she said to herself, let it be on an open mountain slope in my more natural habitat. I will have some space to maneuver out there and can fight a better fight. Let the condor come and I will engage him as best I can, but let it be out there on the open slopes where I will feel more at my ease.

Her pace was measured at first as she moved gently through the underbrush, gasping from pain with each footfall, shuffling and mincing her gait as she tried to break free from the congestion of the lower streambed. One foot first and then the other, now and then a pause to regain her focus, inch by inch, step by step she struggled up along the sharply sloping banks, slipping at times but never falling, desperately trying to maintain her balance so as not to further damage the injured ribs.

She had noticed a small shelf about one third up the side of the canyon wall, no more than a shallow band of rock and had decided that it would be there on that narrow ledge where she would make her final stand. But it would not be easy. The pain was rising now and the mere act of breathing had become a burden. And she was exhausted, too tired to even eat. Nonetheless, she pushed upward through the ravel of brush until at last she broke out into the more open expanse of the canyon's lower meadows.

At once the world opened up for her as she crossed over into the small patch of rolling grassland. It was a rare day, sparkling and clear as the pale glow of morningtide washed across the hillsides. Everything gleamed golden in the breaking dawn and the sky was cloudless and bright. It was much warmer there in the open space away from the shadows and she felt better, allowing herself a few minutes then to savor the more spacious setting of the tiny meadowland, gladdened to have finally escaped from the darkness below. But the pleasure of the moment quickly passed as she glanced up and noticed the return of the shadow of the condor, emerging now from the dim space beyond the canyon rim, darker and larger as it began to rapidly descend.

Downward it came, swinging diagonally back and forth, rising and dropping to the rhythm of the currents of the canyon wind, looping and soaring but always moving downward, drawing ever closer, until finally she could vaguely perceive the features of its face; and the aspect was frightening. The large bird was rapt as if in a trance, eyes fixed straight ahead fiercely glaring in the dim light, still tracking her after all these days, relentless in the hunt and she knew it would soon attack.

She was aware that she must hasten her pace and gain the rock ledge as soon as possible or she had not a chance—the hillside was far too steep to mount an adequate defense and she desperately needed to find more level ground. So she quickened her stride, pushed through all the pain and scurried up the rocky slopes as best she could, finally arriving at the small outcropping of rock just as the sun began to rotate up towards its zenith.

She knew that the condor would have seen her slip and fall, no doubt, but he also would have lost sight of her while she was buried down in the shadows at the bottom of the canyon. And he must have wavered, she mused to herself as she stood there shivering on the thin ledge of rock, must have wondered if she had perished from the force of the fall; must have conceded the possibility that he had wasted all those days and all his precious energy tracking her down—and all for nothing if she were in fact dead.

She delighted in the thought of it, took pleasure in imagining the plight of the starving vulture as he pondered the fate of the young guanaco, wondering to himself if he should simply forsake the venture and go hunt elsewhere. Her mind was rocking gently in pleasant contemplation of his discomfort when she was abruptly shaken from her reverie by a strange whirring sound from off in the distance and as she looked skyward she saw that the huge bird had tucked his wings and was plunging toward her, his great mass plummeting from the heavens like a meteor and she knew at once that he was going to try and slay her in one furious stroke.

He was awkward at it, however. Condors were not birds of prey, were vultures and scarcely endowed with any ability to attack from the air. But it had been a lean season for him and his hunger had driven him far beyond the pale of ordinary reason; he desperately needed to feed and so he kept coming, mercilessly swooping down from the heavens. Beatrice by now was numb to everything about her, could only watch in curious detachment as the enormous bird plunged ever downward. I think that he will probably kill me, she said to herself, and there is not much that I can do, but I will at least kick and bite and try to defend myself; nonetheless, in the deep places of her heart she felt that she was doomed.

The condor's eyes were rolling wildly now as it kept dropping down, half crazed he seemed, diving headlong through the thin mountain air. It was a strange sight, vaguely absurd as the tiny, bare head pushed forward leading the black hulk of the bird's massive body ever downward. Careening now with the odd fleshy growth from its forehead flapping in the wind, tumbling earthward, the bird kept coming and coming, out of control, gaining speed by the second, falling helplessly from the sky.

Beatrice was dazed by it all, insensate, pain surging everywhere through her frail and damaged body as the condor, apparently devoid of reason by now, kept plunging heedlessly downward in his attempt to kill her. She could but watch in abstract fascination and wait, hoping that whatever happened would be over quickly and painlessly. So she calmly wedged her hind shank against the wall of the rock ledge and braced herself for the impact.

But the big bird was far off the mark, was not even close as his huge body swung to the right and smashed into the rock wall several yards from where she stood. The snap of the condor's neck and the crunch of his bones as he slammed into the cliff side resounded across the sunlit slopes, rose up from the silent depths of the canyon and filled the air with the sound of instant death. The crushed body of the hapless condor clung to the face of the rock wall for several seconds and then slid lifelessly to the ground, settling into a pulp of shattered bone and flesh not five feet from where she was standing.

Beatrice was stunned by the sudden confluence of events—the bird had swooped out of the sky like a comet and collided with the wall in a crash that had caused the very mountainsides to tremble; and now he was dead. She was shaking uncontrollably, rooted to the spot where she stood, unthinking, and it was there she remained for a long while until her senses at last began to slowly come around. She had been spared and she was both grateful and relieved, but there was scant solace to be had up there on the windswept face of that canyon wall as she once again began to consider her circumstance.

There was, however, nothing much that she could really do and she knew it. The sun was rotating further to the west and the coldness of late afternoon had begun to settle across the mountainsides. The condor lay directly in front of her, its crushed head twisted upward toward the deepening sky, the eyes remaining curiously open, glassy and gleaming from their splintered sockets, staring blankly up into the Andean sky. The bird had been thoroughly quashed from the impact with the rock wall and was awash in its own blood, glowing crimson now in the low rays of the fading sun.

The carcass of the dead vulture was like an omen to her, an augury of her own demise; yet she knew that her family would never abandon the search, knew that they would continue looking for her until they had all dropped from the effort. But the day was on the wane now, the light quickly fading. I will be much more visible if I am standing, she said to herself, so I shall stay on my feet until every trace of daylight has disappeared. But she knew that it would not be easy.

She had eaten nothing since the night of the great storm and she was so desperately weary, exhausted to the core, but she knew that if she lay down she would never again rise. So she braced herself against the rock wall and dug in, determined to bear with it until the last vestige of light had finally vanished. And all the while she gazed out toward a horizon that was growing dimmer with each passing minute, searching desperately for her family, scanning the distant plateau and hoping.

The shadows were deepening now as the wind began to rise and it was grim for her, rocking back and forth up there on that thin ledge of rock, ceaselessly sweeping the skyline, chilled and trembling. And then quite suddenly she caught sight of a familiar contour rising slowly out of the dim mist on the far horizon, moving cautiously, a distant image it was, long and slender, vaguely rendered in the blue haze of the Andean twilight. And she knew at once that it was her mother, knew it like some primeval whisper from the heart.

The lone figure moved slowly closer as it emerged from the haze and finally came into focus, now assuming the full form of an adult guanaco, the long neck leading forward, probing and bobbing. And it was her mother; of that she was now certain. And then she noticed that the rest of the clan was following close behind, all of them, moving slowly closer to the rim directly opposite from where she stood. She immediately pushed away from the rock face and struggled forward, faltering now as she tenuously approached the rim of the stone precipice, desperate in her effort to be seen.

She began to bleat and whine as loud as her weakened body would allow, swaying back and forth and braying, bellowing to the limits of her strength until finally she noticed the head of her mother snap suddenly to the left and stare straight down to where she teetered precariously on the thin band of rock. And she knew that she had been spotted, knew it immediately and understood at once that she would not die that night. She was too tired to nod in recognition, however, too tired even to lift her head, could but kneel down cautiously onto the rock ledge beneath the brow of the scarp where she gently rolled over and collapsed into herself.

She glanced briefly upward one last time and saw that her mother had begun to pick her way down the canyon side, slowly and carefully, moving steadily toward the ledge of rock where Beatrice lay and she knew she would surely survive, would live to once again enter into the gentle embrace of family and friends. She smiled to herself and gently sighed, a low and plaintive sound that was lost in the swirling canyon winds, then tucked her head down between her forelegs and patiently awaited their arrival, knowing that all would soon be well again.

ALFRED THE PYTHON

It would be a long pilgrimage. Long and difficult. The black waters of the Lualaba flowed silently beneath the limb on which he lay, rushing down through the soft tangle of foliage that spilled over from its shores. The slow heat of central Africa penetrated into every corner of the Congo Basin, seeped down into the darkness beneath the forest canopy and smothered the land; induced a torpor that caused all creatures within its reach to patiently abide until the passing of the zenith of the sun.

In the midst of it all, Alfred the Python was draped over the branch of a massive Mangrove tree cautiously measuring his options, pondering the journey that lay before him, wondering if he would ever be able to rescue the delicate Daphne Dee, light and love of his reptilian life, the adorable Daphne Dee who had been shamefully kidnapped by evil white hunters the week before.

That day had been a bad one for Alfred. Never before had he encountered such strange looking creatures as those ashen faced men who had emerged suddenly out of the shadows of the bush—alien in every aspect they were. Not only did they walk upright balanced on two legs, much more erect it seemed to Alfred than the great apes he had so often seen, but their bodies were wrapped in cloth and their feet bound in hard leather casings. Indeed, they were queer looking in every way and Alfred immediately feared for the impending consequence of their presence.

He had been resting on one of the upper branches of the Mangrove while Daphne Dee, his faithful lover and constant companion for many years, was sprawled below at her ease on one of the lower limbs. They were both glutted to the teeth as the remains of two giant forest hogs roiled and churned in their distended abdomens, both of them completely and sublimely inert as they slowly digested the unfortunate pigs.

The three white men, ugly by any standard that Alfred had come to respect, pounced on poor Daphne Dee without warning. They were a remarkable group, or so it seemed to Alfred, with nets and weapons and spikes, screaming and yelping and cursing as they fell upon the unsuspecting lady and pried her loose from the branch where she was peacefully snoozing. They used prongs and iron bars, snares and loops, long wooden poles and almost anything else they could lay their hands on in an effort to shake the lady loose; nonetheless, she did not go gently, not by any means and it had been a fearsome struggle.

She had not been able to flee—they had swooped down too quickly; all that she could really do was tighten her grip on the branch of the Mangrove, which is what she did, squeezing until her eyeballs bulged nearly loose from their sockets. But it was useless. The protuberance of the half-digested pig was a serious hindrance, caused her to lose her balance and consequently slacken her hold. She was, as well, half paralyzed with lethargy as her body diverted most of its resources toward the digestion of the hapless hog and so she really wasn't at her best. Nonetheless, she did not succumb easily and it took a massive effort to dislodge her from the tree.

But she had no chance really—none at all. After thirty minutes of twisting and grunting and grousing, the men finally managed to wrest her to the ground and while the encounter had been brief, it had been arduous and Daphne Dee was depleted; too tired to even hiss. And so the pale faced demons, grumbling and groaning and spewing profanities all the while, were at last able to stuff her into a portable bamboo cage which they had carried with them for that very purpose. Alfred, safely concealed in the shadows of the tree's upper limbs, was saddened onto tears, could but watch and silently weep as he viewed the disgraceful proceedings. The three men then shunted her off into the dim shadows of the forest, disappearing as quickly as they had come.

Daphne Dee was compelled to lay motionless on the wooden floor of the malodorous bamboo cage, completely exhausted from the effort of the struggle. She was bewildered and dismayed, confused by it all and at once began to coo and lisp in the plaintive tones characteristic of an aggrieved female python. The space was confined, measuring only two feet by five, and she was forced to squeeze herself into a compact and uncomfortable coil, a tight knot of compressed flesh that was causing her to become cramped and nauseous.

It was, to be sure, a dismal circumstance and she was beginning to sink into a deep and potentially terminal funk. Nonetheless, just before entering into the darkness beneath the forest's crown she had glanced up one last time and glimpsed the familiar glint of Alfred's cold and remorseless eye, the indomitable eye of a species that had endured for millions of years and she knew that he would never rest until he had tracked down the scurrilous evildoers and rescued her; and the thought of it calmed her trembling heart.

Alfred, unfortunately, was not able to give chase, could but lie there in tumescent languor as his digestive organs continued to dissolve the giant pig; and it was a torment for him knowing that the cowardly intruders would have such a long head start. It would be another week or so before he would be able to move again, he knew, for he had dined upon these wild boars before and it was always a lengthy process.

He even attempted to regurgitate the pig in an effort to clear his system and once again become mobile; but it was futile. The partially emulsified boar had become integrated into his digestive tract by now and poor Alfred was more or less obligated to lie there helplessly slung across the upper branches of the stately Mangrove; lie there in a soporific stupor and wait it out. Nonetheless, in spite of it all, he remained confident that he would be able to save his beloved Daphne Dee; knew in his heart that his hour would come.

One week later the huge pig had finally been digested. The long wait had been an ordeal for Alfred, an agony as he lay there comatose through it all, barely stirring, patiently contemplating the gurgle and churn of his own gastric juices. But it was all over now; the boar had been successfully converted into latent reservoirs of energy and as he slowly began to slither down through the branches of the Mangrove he could think of nothing but the plight of the lithesome and lovely Daphne Dee, the inexorably delectable Daphne Dee, love of his life.

What could they possibly want with her, he wondered? What good is a big snake to anyone, he pondered? Nonetheless, though his brain was but the size of an average pea, he understood that these haggard looking, fallow faced fiends were evil to the core; knew it like an imprint on his heart and was anguished. And so as he carefully wound his way down the trunk of the great tree and gently slipped into the black waters of the Lualaba, he realized that he could not tarry.

The challenge that lay before him was formidable, however. Alfred lived in the Congo Basin, a vast shallow depression in the heart of central Africa that covered more than 1,300,000 square miles. It was a land of dense equatorial rain forests and murky swamps, a hot, humid expanse of jungle that steamed and weltered through every month of every year on into eternity. Alfred lived on the banks of the big river that flowed through it all, known as the Lualaba in its upper reaches in the Shaba region of the country and finally called the Congo as it emerged from its great bend at Kisangani and rolled out toward the sea.

Alfred, of course, knew nothing of these names bestowed upon the river by other creatures; he knew it only as a great channel of water that cut through the jungles of his native land and flowed out toward the rim of the universe, never ending as it wound its way on toward the stars as far as he knew. But he had heard of a large settlement near the great arc of the river, a place inhabited by curious looking, bipedal, forest dwelling creatures and he sensed intuitively that his beloved Daphne Dee must have been carried there.

Nonetheless, the journey down the Lualaba would be perilous. The river moved swiftly in its upper reaches, plunged rapidly downward across a long chain of plateau escarpments, slicing through narrow gorges and crashing over a succession of steep cascades. Alfred himself had never ventured much beyond the confines of his native hunting grounds, was ill informed about the terrain outside his natural domain, but Franklin the Orangutan, a good friend of his and inveterate traveler, had told him of the many dangers that lurked in the dark waters below.

Alfred was a mature python, 18 feet in length and weighing well over 300 pounds and could easily be crushed by his own body weight should he happen to tumble into any one of the cascades that lay in wait along the way; or he could simply drown. He would need to respond to the winnow and flow of the river, would need to react quickly and slide off toward the margins of the forest every time he sensed the presence of fast water or he would surely be done for. And the cataracts were but one amongst a series of dangers.

The great river was also thick with predators along its varied course, but especially so in the sparsely settled regions near its origins. There were numerous tribes scattered throughout the area and while Alfred had never encountered any of them personally, Franklin had told him that these people did not take kindly to pythonic intruders and were more or less inclined to slay them on the spot, a discouraging thought for a kind hearted reptile like Alfred.

Even more dangerous, however, were the crocodiles, mortal enemy of all pythons everywhere, primordial purveyors of evil and creatures of unrestrained appetites. And Alfred knew that they would be skulking along the riverbanks, laying in wait, poised to lash out and snap him down in the flash of a serpent's tongue. He was well acquainted with the sinister crocs, had done battle with them before, and he knew that they would be lurking everywhere along the river's edge.

For the time being, however, he was safe, moving easily through the calm waters along a languid stretch of the river near the village of Kongolo in the eastern part of the Congo. Pythons were renowned throughout Africa as excellent swimmers and Alfred was no exception as he glided smoothly through this part of the river, cutting like a blade through the gently coursing waters. The Lualaba flowed peacefully here and so he was able to shift his track more toward the middle of the channel where he could move at his ease, swiftly swimming downstream.

He swam with his head arched out above the surface of the water and while he felt relatively secure along this section, he never allowed his concentration to waver, continually casting a wary eye from side to side, constantly sweeping the shorelines for any trace of danger. Nonetheless, he was cruising easily, taking great pleasure in the supple movement of his huge body as it undulated gracefully and efficiently down through the docile currents.

Alfred, pea brained or not, knew that he had embarked upon a treacherous journey, unwieldy and dangerous, understood well that prospects for a successful conclusion were tenuous at best; for not only did he have to rescue his lady love, he also had to escort her safely back to their homeland, a formidable task under the best of circumstances. But he was, for the moment, singularly disinterested in the logistics of the venture, his thoughts focused only on his beloved Daphne Dee, light of his life, and he was determined to rescue the his lady regardless of any attendant perils.

Franklin had told him of the rapacious bands of pusillanimous pasty faced predators who from time to time swept through the jungles and gathered up collections of animal species—lions, leopards, zebras, elephants, water buffaloes and everything else including pythons—and Alfred solemnly envisioned the dark enclave of some cruel menagerie, an assemblage of forlorn specimens from all corners of the Congo Basin, huddled in collective misery while their bilious, bug eyed captors reveled late into the African night.

And in his mind's eye he could envision the delicate Daphne Dee cramped into the dim cavity of some rude and brutish bamboo cage, coiled there in melancholy repose, hissing mournfully into the night. The image of it all burned down into the hidden corners of his tiny reptilian heart, caused the bile to rise from his diminutive reptilian liver and gave him a serious case of indigestion. No misfortune could ever be so ghastly, he said to himself as he belched his way downstream, no stroke of fate so heinous or grave and he was deeply aggrieved.

Nonetheless, he knew he had to get on with it. And he was gliding now, oscillating his long, thick body from side to side, swinging gently to the tempo of the quickening stream. He was moving rapidly, making very good time indeed as the indolent flow of the Kasongo section of the river began to give way to swifter waters. The sound initially arose as a soft roar, an indistinct purling of waters from afar. Alfred paid little heed at first, thought it was nothing more than the rustle of the wind as it sifted down through the tops of the big trees. He was mindful only of the plight of his beloved Daphne Dee, dwelled solely upon the circumstance of her scandalous abduction and was but vaguely aware of the low rumble in the distance.

But it was the sound rising up from the great cataracts below Kibumbo, a frothing, boiling stretch of jagged rock and broken cliffs that devoured anything and everything that washed over into its maw. It was a maelstrom of churning, roiling white water that was utterly inviolate, well beyond the navigational capabilities of any python and over the years had become a cauldron of death for man and beast alike.

By now the channel of the river had narrowed and the rush of water had begun to accelerate. Alfred, engrossed with the task at hand, did but scarcely note the nuance of change in the flow of the river. He only knew that he was cruising now, slipping through the water with consummate ease, moving along faster than he had ever moved before; knew well that time was of the essence and was pleased with his pace. Around a long, looping bend, still cruising, torqueing his huge body through the water with precision and finesse, but moving much faster now.

Alfred, however, like all snakes everywhere was hard of hearing, could, in fact, barely discern frequencies of sound in the upper ranges nor those borne through the air, was ill disposed and poorly prepared to recognize the escalating roar. The rumble of the great cataract kept building of course, intensified with every passing second, until finally the crescendo of the thunder of the falls came crashing down into his consciousness all at once. But by then it was too late.

The roar was absolute by now, filling the air and echoing out across the river and through the forest with a force of its own. Alfred had come up out of the water in order to evaluate the situation, had nearly one third of his body length arced out over the stream, and was dismayed by what he saw. Up ahead bursts of white water were billowing everywhere across the surface of the river and he could begin to glimpse the leading edge of the initial breech of the falls. The water was raging now, whirling and churning all about him, sweeping him along in its vortex like a broken twig, powerful beyond anything he had ever experienced before. And poor Alfred was hopelessly trapped out there in the middle of the channel with no chance at all to gain the shore, swirling helplessly in the great churl of water as it plunged inevitably toward the precipice.

I am surely a goner he said to himself as he hurtled relentlessly forward. He was tumbling now, spinning and twisting from side to side as his huge body began to swing out of control. Above all else he knew that he must keep his head up out of the water or he would surely be doomed, but it wasn't easy. The great bulk of his carcass was spiraling wildly through the water, flipping him over on his back and looping itself into braids as the torrent of the water spumed and crashed all about him. He could really do nothing more than try to maintain some sense of equilibrium and sanity, try to keep from drowning before he was swept over the rim of he falls; but the circumstance was dire and he knew it.

He was completely surrounded by the churn of the frothing waters, absolutely engulfed in the chaos of it all and as he spun out over the lip of the scarp he felt as if he were plunging into some great, dark hole at the bottom of the end of the world. He had by now completely given himself over to the force of the river, realized that he could really do nothing more than patiently abide and so relaxed as best he could and muttered a silent adieu to his beloved Daphne Dee.

He fully anticipated that he would be crunched to a pulp amongst the boulders and spars of sharp rock that lay in wait down at the floor of the falls, cut to shreds in the labyrinth of accumulated detritus that had for eons been carried down over the edge of the falls—splintered logs, shards of stone and bone, tree trunks and all the other assorted stubble that arrived from the world above. So he was curiously calm and detached as his great serpentine length decanted from the main channel of the stream, looping over the brink and spiraling downward toward oblivion. And then something quite rare and extraordinary happened.

His huge, sinuous body, which up to now had whipped and twisted itself into a contortion of knots and bows, began to spontaneously untangle and roll into a big ball; a very big ball to be sure, but nonetheless spherical in its essence, something akin to a great, fleshy coil. He was spinning now rather than spiraling, rotating downward like a big wheel and when at last he crashed against the first large boulder into a fume of exploding water, he bounced instead of splatted.

How strange, he said to himself, as he sprang upward and out instead of back down into the froth of water and jagged rock; how utterly extraordinary. And so it was that he continued on downward, bounding and bouncing, skipping and glancing through the maze of dross that had accumulated in the stream bed over centuries of rain and runoff, caroming on down through the cascade like a giant rubber ball.

Alfred was confounded by it all, could really do nothing more than clench his teeth and protect his head, which he did by tucking it under one of the inner folds of coiled flesh. Onward and downward through the great chasm below Kibumbo, ricocheting from boulder to boulder as he rolled through the fierce rapids; bouncing and flying around like a tennis ball caught in a hurricane. But it was no glide through the jungle—not by any means. He could hear his ribs cracking and snapping with every concussion, could feel the squishing of his flesh as he slammed into the big rocks, and it was a torment for him.

Nonetheless, as long as he didn't crush his head he sensed he might have a chance to survive, knew that at 18 feet in length he could well afford to sacrifice a few ribs here and there—so he closed his eyes and simply rolled with the flow. And when he finally emerged into the more placid waters beneath the falls, he could feel that his heart was still beating, could feel his body contracting in and out as it continued to breathe and so he knew he was not yet dead.

He was, nonetheless, battered and bruised as he floated out into the still waters of the great pool beneath the rapids. His long body had reverted to its normal, serpentine configuration as the muscles finally relaxed, releasing the enormous coil of flesh that had enabled him to survive. Curiously, however, most of him had escaped undamaged as the outer band had absorbed most of the punishment with the inner rings remaining in tact, virtually unmarked. But he ached terribly through his upper torso, could barely keep his head up out of the water as he slowly swung his mangled thighs from side to side, winding his way across the deep pool on over toward the river's edge.

Eventide had begun to settle across the junglelands by now and the screeching of the night birds began to rise up from the darkness within; the air was verily pulsing with peril as the predators of early evening prepared themselves for the hunt. Nonetheless, Alfred knew that he would need to pass the night here near the fringe of the riverbank close to the cusp of the forest, understood well that he would need to rest his broken body before he could continue on.

Yet, in spite of all, in spite of the pain and nausea and general discomfort, his thoughts returned once more to his beloved Daphne Dee and he nearly swooned in the contemplation of her loveliness—the gentle hiss and delicately flicking tongue, the tenderness of her smoothly scalloped scales, the lilt of her hooded eyes. The memory of her enduring beauty caused his miniscule reptilian heart to palpitate wildly, caused him to momentarily forget the discomfort of his own circumstance and once again reminded him that he must struggle onward at any cost in order to rescue her. Nonetheless, he was exhausted and it was only with the greatest of effort that he gained the edge of the forest floor and slowly pulled his ponderous bulk into the sanctuary of a nearby copse of orchids.

As he lay there in the encroaching darkness, his mind drifted back to an earlier time, another time many years before when he had suffered a comparable travail. He had been hunting in the wooded marshlands along the upper basin of the big river, cruising silently through the papyrus and sedge, searching for herons and storks and anything else that could appease his considerable hunger. The water was the color of black tea back in the sloughs and glades of the Lualaba outwash and he could more or less glide along at his leisure there, undetectable in the shallow pools of dark water.

It was late twilight and the moon was full that night, was, in fact, even now beginning to cast a sallow glow across the steaming marshes. There was, as always, a heavy mist hanging over the wetlands, thick and silent, a dim cloud of humid air which served to muffle the sporadic sounds of the night hunters that had begun to filter in from the surrounding forests. Alfred was well aware that he had entered into the realm of the great crocodiles of the upper Congo, grim and vigilant predators of the marshes along the river's edge, but the hunting could be good back in the wallows midst the misty sloughs, very good indeed, and so he had been willing to risk it.

And ordinarily there would have been no problem; but on this particular night the wash of light from the ascending moon had betrayed him, had provided enough illumination to limn the profile of his upper body as it arched out over the flat expanse of water. The huge crocodile exploded out of the nearby mud bank as if it had been suddenly purged from the viscera of some primeval sludge, surged forward in a rage, serrated teeth gleaming in the pale light of the rising moon, and clamped its powerful jaws into the mid section of Alfred's submerged trunk.

He never saw it coming, sensed only the flurry of water as the croc burst up from the shadows and locked its mighty jaws onto his girth, heard the crack of snapping ribs and felt the gush of blood, but in the essence of it was taken fully by surprise. The crocodile secured its hold and then began to twist and spin, spiraling up out of the water in a frenzy, flailing away furiously in an effort to drag Alfred down below the surface and drown him; wrenched and shook the big snake with all the strength he could summon from his ancestral instincts. But he had struck too low on the python's body, had allowed him too much freedom and flexibility in the upper reaches of his long torso and so could not immediately pull him under.

Alfred had instantly begun to weave and bob back and forth, desperately swinging his head and upper body from side to side as he tried to stay above the water's plane. It was a mortal encounter between two creatures who had both evolved from the tidal pools and smoking ash of ancient earth; and it was fearsome. Alfred had managed to wrap the crocodile into his powerful coil, but the huge reptile was implacable, continued to writhe and gyrate in atavistic fury, at times balancing on his tail and coming up out of the water in a nearly vertical stance as Alfred continued to squeeze with all the strength that he could draw from his wounded body.

But the crocodile was a serious adversary, a large, voracious male, and it was a daunting struggle for the both of them. Alfred, of course, knew nothing of his own mortality, knew nothing of death as a natural consequence of his existence, but he did understand that his very survival depended upon his capacity to endure for awhile, to persevere and respond in kind and he was fully prepared to fight to the end.

But the croc was truly formidable, had long ago matured into a deadly and efficient killer who was not to be easily denied that night. And so the two ancient enemies battled, one against the other, locked together in a lethal embrace down along the marshes of the Lualaba in the deepest heart of the Congo Basin. The fight proceeded in cycles—great spasms of energy interspersed with extended periods of rest and eerie silence—but always, even during the lapses of inactivity, Alfred was compelled to keep his head above the water's edge, dipping and swaying as the crocodile hung tenaciously to his belly.

After several hours of unremitting combat, Alfred could feel his strength begin to ebb, could see the dark stain of his own blood seeping out from the jaws of the croc and spilling over into the turbid waters of the sough, glowing amber now in the light of the ascendant moon; could feel his strength slowly drain away as he desperately strove to maintain his grip.

And then quite suddenly, or so it had seemed to Alfred at the time, the crocodile's hold began to loosen, an ever so slight lessening of tension that Alfred could feel through the span of his long body. He sensed intuitively that the croc was beginning to tire, could feel it down in the deepest reaches of his instincts and realized that it was only a matter of time now. He at once tightened his coil, slowly began to constrict the powerful muscles throughout his serpentine length, drew from every resource of his reptilian being and methodically began to squeeze the life from the obdurate crocodile.

He had been able to measure the heartbeat of the croc, could feel along the course of his finely tuned torso the waning of his pulse and so he knew that he was fading, knew that he would soon succumb. And then he felt the body go slack, felt the jaws relax and release their grip and he knew that the implacable croc had finally gone under. Alfred slowly loosened the tension on his coil and surrendered the lifeless creature to the dark waters of the marsh, watched in silent contemplation as it slid down into the muck at the bottom of the wallow.

He had returned home that night, the pain from the open gash surging through the length of his body as he sidled carefully along the fringe of the forest's edge, arriving at long last into the tender embrace of the delicate Daphne Dee. She had nursed him back to health that year, patiently tending to the grievous wound, had, in fact, saved his life by virtue of her loving care and now as he lay there in the orchid grove beneath the roar of the great falls below Kibumbo he knew that he must let nothing deter him in his effort to rescue her; neither cascades nor crocodiles nor frenzied white hunters—nor anything.

And he also realized in the remembrance of that fatal encounter that he could indeed endure; above all else had learned that he had the capacity to push through the direst of circumstance. So he rested that night, allowed his damaged body to begin to mend itself, slept deeply under the starlit veil of orchids as visions of the delicate Daphne Dee slithered through his dreams.

He awakened the next morning just as the first light of dawn began to filter down through the forest canopy. The heat was oppressive, as always, and he hurt all over, ached from tongue tip to tail, but he paid scant heed to any of it; for he knew he could not linger, could not tarry for even an instant if he wished to reclaim his lover and lifelong companion, the indescribable Daphne Dee. So he plunged back into the river and immediately made his way over to the middle of the channel, only this time he set a moderate pace, proceeded with considerably more prudence than before.

He had learned a few things from the ordeal of the previous day, was more sensitive now to the nuance of the river, more conscious of the swirl and fleck of the surface of the stream, for he was aware that he could never survive another pounding the likes of which he had absorbed the day before; knew that he had been carried away by his passion and pervading love for Daphne Dee—had allowed his emotions to preempt his pythonic good judgment and he could not let it happen again.

But the river was much more subdued in this section, ran flat and smooth and so he was able to cruise along effortlessly. Down past Kindu and Lowa, undulating easily through the quiescent waters now, onward past Ubundi where he traversed over into the forest's edge in order to circumvent the cataracts at Stanley Falls, far steeper and much more violent than those at Kibumbo, a holocaust of bursting, churning white water that swallowed up anything and everything that encroached into its range. He was obliged to detour around these mighty falls at Stanley and it had cost him some time, one full day in fact, for he was a large and cumbersome creature and could move but slowly through the tangle of jungle vegetation.

But he was patient and disciplined in the finest tradition of reptilian creatures everywhere and so managed to struggle through, eventually reentering the river well below the egress of the rapids. He hastened along as best he could to make up for lost time and at long last arrived at the outskirts of Kisangani just as the twilight of early evening had begun to settle across the great bend of the river. The journey from the orchid grove below Kibumbo had taken three full days and nights during which time he had neither slept nor rested and he was very tired. Nonetheless, he knew he could not tarry.

Kisangani was a large settlement, ugly and onerous by any criterion imposed by the aesthetically sensitive Alfred, and the search for Daphne Dee would be difficult; nonetheless, there were some clues and indications. First, the depraved creatures who had abducted her were all white men living in an overwhelmingly black community and would necessarily be conspicuous. Second, they would have had to construct their compound on the periphery of the village in order to accommodate the wide range of species that they had recently kidnapped, therefore effectively eliminating the central areas of town.

Third, the white devils would be drinking heavily, as was their wont according to Franklin the Orangutan, would be juiced to the gills no doubt, blustering raucously long into the night and so would be easily detectable. Lastly, and most importantly perhaps, Alfred would be able to taste the presence of Daphne Dee in the air with repeated flicks of his highly attuned tongue—the subtle bouquet of her reptilian body oils, the succulent fragrance of the recently digested wart hog on her breath—all of it would hang in the tumid air of the Congo Basin like the blossom of a freshly bloomed rose; and so, with his delicately tempered tongue probing in and out, he commenced his search and was able to locate the encampment within a few hours.

It was a strange place. There were cages strewn about everywhere, all of them containing specimens of every size and species from spider monkeys to gorillas, each animal hopelessly imprisoned behind the rough-hewn stakes of the primitive pens. In spite of the vast assemblage of life spread out across that open field, an eerie and unseemly silence hung everywhere throughout the compound; a kind of deathly pall. The area was dimly lit, but Alfred could see inside most of the cages and the aspect of it all caused him to gasp in disbelief.

Every one of the animals, without exception, was huddled into the sullied corner of its respective pen staring blankly out into the African darkness, disconsolate and heartsick, all of them, from the frenetic jackal to the naturally lethargic three toed sloth. It was a mournful and scandalous scene and Alfred silently wept as he beheld the sorry spectacle. The only source of light came from a small, wooden hut in the center of the encampment, a rude, hastily rendered structure that contained one large room.

The entire space was screened off and everything inside was visible, as if the occupants paid little heed nor were particularly concerned with the proceedings beyond their rustic hovel. There were several cots scattered about and a big table at the center where Alfred was able to easily discern the grisly silhouettes of three unsightly white men as they entered into another night of shameless and unrestrained debauchery.

But, in truth, he was disinterested in the three hunters, felt no need for vengeance, harbored no grudges as such and wished them no ill will, despicable though they may be. He wanted only to find Daphne Dee and flee; just that and nothing more. And so he began to slide quietly through the maze of cages, shifting his great bulk carefully from side to side so as not to cause any alarm amongst his brethren, tongue flicking in and out as he tasted the air, diligently tracking the scent of the delicate Daphne Dee.

He moved warily and with great circumspection, always watchful, glancing up frequently to review the disposition and demeanor of the three fools inside the hut. But they were otherwise occupied and so he continued advancing steadily forward, gently rotating his huge hips as the scent grew ever stronger. Above all else, he did not want to startle any of the captive animals since any kind of commotion, anything out of the ordinary rising from the loose circle of cages would surely shake the white demons from their drunken reveries.

In particular he worried about the monkeys, high strung and skittish by nature it seemed to the unflappable Alfred, for once one of the nervous little simians went off the other animals would join in and the ensuing tumult would be enough to waken half of Africa; and so the process was agonizingly slow. But the scent grew ever more piquant with each passing second and he knew that he was closing in, past the lions and baboons, silently slithering through the labyrinth of wooden pens, tongue flicking in and out, sensing he was drawing close; and then he spotted her.

Tears immediately welled up into his hooded reptilian eyes and his little heart nearly exploded. There she was, coiled into a tight spiral back in the dank recesses of the very same cage in which she had been captured, irresistible still even in the midst of all the squalor in that fetid pen. She was lying there softly wheezing in the slop and slime of that vile enclosure, motionless and virtually comatose, an appalling sight to behold.

Her color had faded into a deathly gray and her breathing was shallow, barely perceptible—and she had lost a woeful amount of weight. Alfred began to sob uncontrollably at the sight of her, heaving and moaning, despairing of it all as he gazed upon the divine Daphne Dee, the incomparable Daphne Dee, love of his reptilian life, lying there in abject misery. Have these white devils no sense of decency, he muttered to himself, have they no shame, and he was at once both grief stricken and enraged.

She seemed to be sleeping and so he softly cooed the sibilant hiss of the ancient python mating call in an effort to gently rouse the lady from her slumber. Her head was drooped down into the core of her coil, but as soon as she heard the tender tones of Alfred's familiar love song, she slowly lifted up and peered tentatively out into the dim light of the compound, searching through the darkness until at last the eyes of the two lovers locked, their hearts melting then into one, both of them hissing and flicking in spontaneous eruptions of primordial ardor.

Alfred could barely contain himself, wanted only to rip through the wooden bars of the cage and entwine himself amongst the coils of his little flower, wanted only to braid himself along the length of her svelte and sinuous body, but he knew that they must control themselves or they would surely incite a riot. And so he signaled to her that they must subdue their passion for the time being, with a reverse peristaltic shimmy let it be known that they must cool their fervor until he could formulate a plan.

But it would be a delicate undertaking, for while her spirits had momentarily soared upon seeing her man, she had been deteriorating for some time now and her overall physical condition was in rapid decline; and so Alfred knew he must not allow his resolve to slacken, not for an instant, knew he must break her loose that very night. But his options were limited for she was clearly too weak to help him and so he knew he would have to act alone.

Albert, in truth, was not much given to abstract ruminations and he quickly decided that he would simply have to dismantle the stakes—split, crack, snap or otherwise bring them down by whatever means possible; must somehow fashion a gap sufficiently wide for Daphne Dee to slither through. But he was a snake, both legless and armless, and it would, at best, be a dubious enterprise.

Nonetheless, he at once surmised that the white men would have underestimated the strength and mass of an adult python, would have worried more about the legendary prowess of the lion and gorilla and largely discounted the power of a big snake; the hunters were, in fact, no more than interlopers poaching and plundering through unknown terrain, dilettantes plunging blindly through the darkest corners of a land about which they knew virtually nothing.

He therefore suspected that the stakes used to build the cages for serpents might be less solid, were perhaps a bit more vulnerable than those used for the larger beasts and could therefore be compromised if subjected to some irresistible force, some overpowering concussion, some cataclysmic shock—something like the impact of a rolling python.

For he vividly recalled his descent down through the cataracts when he had been able to coil himself up into a big ball, remembered well the great clap and shudder of his carcass as it bounded down amongst the boulders and he decided that he could do it again—most certainly could do it again to save his beloved Daphne Dee. So he dragged himself up to a small hillock that rose above the flat surface of the prison compound and laboriously began to spin his long body into a massive coil, round and round, finally tucking his head into the outer rim of the last loop as he completed the labor. And so there he was, 300 pounds of quavering snake flesh lying on his side like a huge spool of mottled cable, primed and ready to roll to the rescue.

With one titanic surge he heaved himself up onto his outer rim and began to rotate forward, slowly at first but quickly gaining speed, rolling downward, spinning and turning, plunging toward the crude wooden cage that held Daphne Dee. Onward he spiraled, ever and ever faster, making a great whirring sound as he descended, almost a blur now as he whirled forward.

The impact of his tightly coiled carcass as it struck the row of wooden stakes filled the air and reverberated through the compound with a sound as if the universe itself had exploded; shook the ground and caused the very tree tops to tremble. Splinters of wood went flying everywhere, chunks of timber and scraps of metal sent skimming through the air in all directions as Alfred careened ingloriously back toward the rear of the cage and smashed into the far wall, bouncing off with a thunderous thud and finally coming to rest on top of Daphne Dee.

The entire compound erupted—the monkeys went berserk, screeching and squealing and jumping up and down, the lions began to roar and the hyenas started bawling and squalling as utter bedlam ensued. The force of Alfred's weight as he landed on top of his sweetheart nearly crushed poor Daphne Dee, but she paid it no mind, was conscious only of the fluttering of her heart as she snuggled up to her lover and lifelong mate. They gazed into one another's eyes and sighed, tongues tenderly flicking and noses nuzzling as they slowly began to entwine into one last, desperate reptilian embrace; for they both knew what is coming. Cooing together, slowly braiding, they yielded to their passion, looping gently then one onto the other.

Alfred could feel the vibrations of the hurried footfalls as the white hunters hastened toward the chaotic scene, instantly recognized the hard leather casings of their perpetually bound feet as they planted themselves firmly in front of the shattered cage; wryly noted their soiled khaki shorts and recoiled from the stench of their heavily liquored breath.

And as he lay there blissfully enlaced amongst the coils of the amorous Daphne Dee midst the roar and tumult of the frenzied menagerie, his eyes moved slowly upward, past the rolls of belly fat and sweat stained arm pits, further upward still until at last he glimpsed the deadly glint of steel, knew what was coming and so tightened his coil in one last paroxysm of rapture. And then the sudden flash of gun powder as the crack of the rifle split the night air, then another and another, the shrill peal of gunfire rising above the general clamor, the last sounds that either one of them would ever hear as

Alfred the Python and his life long love Daphne Dee clung each to the other in one last loving embrace.

ISABEL THE BEAR

It would be a long crossing. Long and difficult. She stared out across the enduring river of ice that flowed down from the mountain tops, contemplated the huge glacier as it ground slowly through the long valley and spilled over into the boulder fields below. Out in the distance, far away, the solitary massif of Denali rose up from the surrounding plains, surfaced abruptly from the horizon like some great white whale plowing through an endless firmament.

Thin wisps of snow continually spiraled off the shoulders of the big mountain, constant testimony to the fierce winds that forever raked the upper reaches of Denali. And while the days were still warm and clear in this the season of abiding light, Isabel the Bear knew that the nights would soon grow longer, knew that the weather would deepen and turn long before she arrived on the other side. And she feared for the travail that lay ahead.

The two men had been stalking her now for three days and she was growing weary. They were relentless and she knew that they would never quit the hunt, would track her unto to death if need be. One was a white man, crimson of hue and burly through the shoulders; he moved slowly but with consummate patience, slogging through the scrub and bush of the taiga with a measured, plodding stride. From time to time he would rest, would set his pack to the side and nap awhile, but never for very long. He should have tired by now, Isabel kept thinking to herself; he is heavy and flaccid and it has been three days now that he has been tracking me. But he refused to yield in spite of it all, kept dragging his unseemly corpulence across the immense Alaskan tundra in pursuit of the grizzly bear that had killed his wife.

The other man was an Eskimo, a native Indian of the northlands, and Isabel knew he would track her on to eternity. He was lean and supple, always moving apace, always well in advance of the ruddy faced white man. He cruised easily through the low shrubs of the sparse terrain, skipping softly across the rolling tundra with uncommon agility. He would be a formidable adversary, she knew, an Inuit whose people had been forged from the icy plains and polar winds of the Arctic, a Mongol nomad whose courage and will could never be doubted. Indomitable and steadfast were the natives of the far north and she knew he would follow hard upon her trail until he fell dead from the effort.

They were pursuing her because she had burst into their camp one dark and moonless night and dispatched the woman of the white man; had, in fact, mauled and battered her into a mangle of crushed bone and blood pulp in the fever of her rage. The woman, fair of skin and delicate, unaccustomed it would seem to the ways of the wilderness, had seized Isabel's cub one day not long ago and carried it back to their campsite.

She had taken the young bear inside the tent with her, perhaps to nurture and care for it or perhaps to simply amuse herself for awhile midst the loneliness of the Alaskan bush. Isabel was ignorant of the lady's motives and singularly disinterested. She knew only that her baby had been snatched from her and that she intended to reclaim it by whatever means necessary; knew that much for a fact and meant to remedy the circumstance as soon as possible.

She had given birth to twins the springtime past, a pair of males, but the weaker of the two had been eaten by a vagrant wolf shortly after birth and so she was left with but the one. She had placed the young cub under the protective canopy of an aging willow as she foraged for food one evening, had believed that he was well concealed beneath the thick boughs of the large tree, but upon returning had discovered he was missing. At first she thought that he had but wandered off, was merely exploring the surrounding forestlands or chasing rodents or something of the sort.

But she then detected the pungent odor of a human animal, the acrid essence of the creature who walked upright on two legs; perceived at once the scent of a foreign presence and so immediately began to track it down. It was easy to follow, a strange mixture of perfume and perspiration and feminine body odor that hung in the arctic air like smoke and after several hours of sniffing and probing she finally arrived at an isolated encampment along the banks of a small stream.

She wasted not a second, immediately perceived the shadow of her infant cub mid the sallow glow of a kerosene lamp, recognized her baby and charged straight ahead with not a moment's hesitation. She ripped through the side of the tent as if it were a curtain of cobweb, fell upon the lady and clawed at her with instinctive vengeance, tore her to pieces and then flung her to the side. It was swift and merciless and in the frenzy of it all the young cub was cast aside and had run off into the darkness squealing, forever lost it would seem, as Isabel bellowed and roared into the confusion of the moment.

The mate of the slain woman came running at once, rifle at the fore, screaming wildly and firing from the waist as he plunged into the horror of the scene that greeted him. The Inuit followed closely behind, but seemed oddly indifferent to the slough of carnage strewn out before him, curiously detached and unaffected by the shredded remains of the slaughtered white lady as he lingered in the shadows while the white man decided what to do.

Isabel had been forced to flee, addled and bewildered, bounding through the darkness all alone. She galloped recklessly across the shifting tundra, storming through the arctic night in an anguish of terror as she tried to outdistance the enraged white hunter and his Inuit guide, both of whom had gathered their weapons and given chase in accordance with the white man's wishes. She had in fact been on the run now for three days and three nights and was drained to the bone as she rolled back on her haunch and gazed numbly off into the distance, too frightened to rest yet too exhausted to immediately continue.

Isabel's home was the Alaskan Range and its surrounding environs, the great ridge of mountain crests that rises up from the boreal forests of the arctic and divides the interior tundra prairie from the Pacific Coast ranges. Denali, high one in the Inuit tongue, or Bolshaya Gora, great mountain in the Russian language, is the massive summit that ascends precipitously from the center of the formation, dominating the landscape for hundreds of miles in every direction.

Isabel had roamed the hills and plains adjacent to Denali for all her nine years, had given birth to numerous cubs during that time and knew the land as if it were an imprint on her soul, was intimate with the terrain from the marshy woodlands of the southern slopes to the frozen tundra of the north; had gorged herself on the weasels and lemmings that teemed up from the meadows in the springtime and had fed upon the black crow berries and mushrooms of the juniper forests during the season of the high sun. And she had survived all those long winters during her nine years, curling into the folds of a silent slumber as her pulse slowed to a murmur and her body drew slow nourishment from the thick stores of fat that she had accumulated during the summer season.

Isabel had prowled and hunted that vast mountain hinterland at her leisure, acknowledging no enemies and fearing no presence save the creature who walked upright on two legs; had stalked the wild land with abandon in the course of her time. Indeed, she knew every nuance and roll of the place as no other creature ever could—but she had never crossed over onto the other side, had never seen the coastal ranges nor ever ventured up onto the glaciers and snowfields that straddled the shoulders of the great mountain; knew nothing, really, of the higher elevations up near the ridgelines. And so she was anxious and vaguely apprehensive as she approached the ice fields that loomed in the distance.

She did, however, know that she dare not tarry; the white man would eventually weaken and fade, of that she was certain, but the Mongol would be unfaltering and so she knew that she must keep moving. She glanced back in an effort to measure the distance between her and the two pursuers, but the brilliance of the noon day sun was blinding and so she turned once again toward the mountain and gazed out across the silent sweep of glacial ice that tapered off toward the distant summits.

It was an infinite swath of snow, treeless and barren, an ocean of white that stretched as far as the eye could manage. Isabel peered out across the immense fields of ice as they veered up to the west and disappeared into the horizon, spent several minutes silently pondering the emptiness of it all, reflecting then upon the gravity and length of the passage that lay ahead.

She had chosen to escape across the mountains because she knew the two men would be poorly equipped to follow her onto the glacier fields. They were hunters, not mountain people, highly skilled in the tracking and killing of other creatures but ill disposed to deal with the desolation and deep cold of higher elevations. All of their weapons and traps and assortment of modern gear would be of little use up there on the snowfields of the big mountain, would do nothing but slow them down. And they would not be carrying much food with them, would have preferred instead to be hunting their meals as they went along, as was their custom, an uncomplicated task in the forests and taigas of the lower valleys, but an impossibility on the sterile slopes of Denali.

If she could but gain the snowline before they killed her she would have an advantage, or so she surmised, as her reservoirs of fat would serve her well at the higher altitudes, would provide adequate nourishment through many cycles of the sun. But the two humans would begin to succumb almost at once, would begin to slowly starve and freeze from the instant they crossed over onto the glacier fields. They would have neither the physical reserves to endure the terrible cold of nighttime nor sufficient cover to withstand the blistering sun of midday as it reflected off the snow and cooked them to cinders out there on the open slopes. And so she knew she had a chance.

She continued weaving her way slowly through the low bush and scrub of the taiga, on upward towards the fringe of the glacier, conserving her energy as best she could. Isabel was a mature grizzly, standing well over six feet and weighing more than eight hundred pounds and while she could achieve speeds of more than thirty miles an hour in sudden bursts, her legs were short and not evolved for endurance; so she needed to pace herself. But here in the transitional zones she fell easily into the rhythms of her natural gait as the shrubs and willow groves of the lower elevations began to give way to gently rolling meadows.

She was very tired but still moving at a steady speed, pushing through the exhaustion, fully aware that once she reached the glacier the going would be much more difficult. Isabel's claws were straight rather than curved, designed for digging and slashing and would be a hindrance up on the granular surface of the snowfields and so she was uneasy as she made her way up higher and higher along the mountain side, knew that she would be entering into an unknown realm and was fearful for what lay ahead. But for the time being she was moving along at a reasonable pace.

Occasionally she would stop and roll her head back to see if she could spot either one of the two men who were tracking her. As the sun circled lower into the western sky, the glare began to diminish and so she was able to vaguely perceive the blurred silhouettes of two distant and indistinct figures; her eyesight was poor and she could but barely glean an image, but she was certain it was them.

The white man was by now dropping further and further behind while the Mongol continued gliding effortlessly through the low shrubs, shifting and slipping across the broad taiga with consummate ease, like a dancer he was, graceful and lithe. And absolutely tireless. But the porcine Caucasian was stopping to rest with ever more frequency and for longer periods of time and she could tell that he was struggling.

He will soon expire, she thought to herself, within the day will fall from exhaustion and die where he lay, for the Mongol will never return to offer succor, will be gladdened in fact to be rid of the burden of his company. The Inuits despised the white man, regarded him as weak and whining, unworthy in every aspect of his pathetic existence and so she was certain the Mongol would let him rot where he dropped.

But the fate of the Caucasian had never much concerned her anyway—he was nothing more than a nuisance at best. It was the inalterable Inuit who was her mortal enemy and always had been, the intrepid Mongol who had become fanatically committed to the chase and would by now be obsessed with the killing of this grizzly bear who had eluded him for three full days, would hunt her down and destroy her or die in the attempt. It was in his blood, a mandate rising up from his ancestral heritage and Isabel knew that he would be unrelenting in his efforts to slay her.

She allowed herself a few minutes rest while she tracked the path of the Indian. He was moving very quickly now, even for an Inuit, and she was disquieted by his pace; this will be the longest and most harrowing of journeys, she said to herself once again, and I will be lucky to survive. But there was really nothing more that she could do but push ahead and so she continued to drag herself upward. From time to time she would glance back to check the progress of the Mongol and she could see that he was slowly gaining ground and so she would try to lengthen her stride, chugging along as fast as her great bulk would allow, continuing to grind her way upward until finally, just as the spectral glow of the Arctic twilight began to wash across the mountainside, she arrived at the glacier's edge and with one great burst of energy leapt up onto the silent fields of snow.

It was all so rare and strange to her, a fallow expanse of ice and snow without a trace of vegetation anywhere—a world bereft of life, scoured clean by wind and cold through eons of time, an austere and empty land that was like nothing she had ever seen before. Far in the distance, too far to contemplate, the upper reaches of the great glacier glimmered in the low light, shimmering softly in the fading twilight; like a dream it was, ethereal in the soft glow of eventide and for one brief instant she was enraptured by the majesty of it all, was awed by the grandeur of the great mountain in spite of the dangers that lay within.

But up close the aspect of the ice field was far more ominous, an alien land of unknown portent, as if she had stumbled over the edge of the earth and plunged into some frozen abyss beyond the reach of time. The surface of the glacier, however, was much more pliant than she had anticipated, was actually a soft cushion of sun ripened snow and much to her surprise did not collapse beneath her considerable mass. And although she could advance but slowly, shuffling one paw forward at a time, she was able to move upward without serious consequence and so continued pulling herself forward for two full days and nights, never resting, upward and upward she hauled her ponderous body across the interminable sea of ice.

At these latitudes during the summer season the sun but barely dipped beneath the horizon during its nocturnal arc and even in the deepest hours of early morning a pale afterglow would cling to the rim of the western sky. She soon discovered that she could travel at a constant pace throughout the complete rotation of the sun, was never constrained by the absence of light and so boldly forged ahead, moving upward through the dim shadows of the sub arctic nights, onward and upward through the heat and searing sun of the daylight hours. But it was not easy.

The cold that invariably settled in during the nighttime hours did not bother her, but in the daytime the intensity of the summer sun beating down through the thin air would drain her of force, would cause her to slacken her pace and move more slowly and she began to wonder then if she could endure. Worse yet, on the evening of the third day she sensed a shift in the wind, noted the darkening skies and churlish stream of clouds that even now had begun to obscure the distant ridgelines.

The auspice was ominous and so she struggled to quicken her pace; but she was exhausted to the core and it was difficult. Nonetheless, she could not and would not pause to rest, for she knew that the Mongol would be gaining ground with every advancing footfall. And so she drove herself onward, doing the best she could, growing weaker and weaker with each passing hour as she moved further and further up the icy slopes of the glacier.

Occasionally she would glance back to see if she could sight the Mongol, but the ice and snow and sky had all melded together into a milky blur and she could discern nothing of a human form. She imagined that he was suffering up there on the snowfields without adequate clothing or nourishment, but she knew as well that he would be moving ahead at a constant pace, closing the distance between them with every stride. As she forced her way on upward her mind would often wander, her thoughts often drifting back to an earlier time, a time some several years ago when she had been hunted down by another Mongol, kinsman to the man tracking her now she supposed—indeed, as they were all kinsmen to one another—and she recalled the tenacity with which he had pursued her.

It had been during the season of the ascendant sun after she had but recently awakened from her long winter's sleep, when she was still torpid and sluggish and struggling to regain her balance. The Inuit, who was only interested in her fur since the flesh of the grizzly was greasy and disgusting to Eskimo people, had followed her then for two days and two nights without surcease; two days and two nights without sustenance or rest. Steady and persistent he was, conceding nothing in the chase, until Isabel had finally backtracked and ambushed him from behind in the ebon hours of early morn when the sun was at its lowest ebb, had fallen upon the Mongol and crushed him in an instant, for he was no match for her in a direct encounter.

But in the memory of it, she understood that she had been compelled to resort to artifice in order to vanquish him, remembered well that she had been exhausted and could not have endured much longer. But that was down in the forests of the lowlands and had been an easy thing to do; up on the open face of the glacier she was hopelessly vulnerable and so she had no choice but to continue to struggle forward, higher and higher up the ice bound valleys of mighty Denali.

For hours and hours in the dim light of the mountain dawn she shuffled forward—one front paw forward and then the other as she dragged it up from behind, over and over in an endless cycle, step by step she pulled herself upward, moving inexorably into the face of the approaching storm. Then, just as she was nearing the 14,000 foot level, the glacier swung abruptly to the left and opened into a vast, circular bowl; it was the headwall of the great divide that separated the Alaskan interior from the Coastal ranges to the west and in that single instant the aspect of the mountain suddenly changed.

Great cliffs of rock and black ice loomed up all around her on all sides, a commanding cirque of snow shrouded peaks and granite pinnacles shimmering golden in the refulgence of the recently risen sun.

Everywhere in all directions there were stone walls and dark crags, fathomless chutes and huge cornices of snow curling up over the lips of the ridgelines—it was a world distinct, a cold, bleak cauldron of ice and snow and shattered rock; and utterly impenetrable.

Isabel immediately understood that she was trapped, that it would be impossible to cross over to the other side. She was enveloped on three flanks by nearly vertical scarps, deep in the shadows of a remote mountain basin with no egress except to the rear from whence the half crazed Mongol would soon arrive. And now the winds had begun to rise, gently at first but steadily building, twisting across the frozen valley with ever increasing velocity until finally they exploded off the mountainsides and came swooping down across the bowl of ice with a virulence like none she had ever seen before. Cross whipping and spiraling from side to side, howling and screaming, they ripped across the glacial surface like a horde of demons risen up from the dark reaches of some distant mountain kingdom and Isabel the Bear despaired for her life—feared from the deepest parts of her being that she was doomed.

Still, she had no option but to continue upward; there was really nothing else that she could do. Should she turn back, the Mongol would surely kill her for she had seen the weapons that the Inuit carried and they were deadly; had seen the power of the long, hollow rods that could drive a shell through the heart of a full grown caribou and she knew that she would be slain if she headed back down the glacier. And so she struggled forward through the maelstrom of whirling snow and ice, on upward toward the head wall that now loomed dark and cold in the distance.

And as the wind roared across the cirque, it began to trigger avalanches from everywhere, crashing down all around her, scores of them booming off the mountainsides. They would release with a sudden crack that split through the alpine air like a rifle shot, a series of thunderous ruptures that spalled off the cliff faces and rumbled out across the valley floor. They were prodigious and devastating, huge torrents of ice and snow that reverberated back up into the heavens with unearthly vehemence and it seemed to Isabel as if the universe itself had begun to burst apart. She was terror stricken by it all, could not even begin to comprehend the power of such events, but nonetheless continued moving upward.

For five hours more she pushed forward into the storm, insensate with weariness by now, on and on through the fury of the high mountain tempest. And then, just as the winds had begun to ease, she stumbled across the bergschrund, the great crevasse that opens up as the glacier separates from the headwall, a gaping cleft that extended from one side of the ice field to the other and on up toward the walls of the cliff face. It was deep and dark and completely impassible, a bottomless canyon of ice and Isabel realized at once that her journey had drawn to a sudden and certain closure, knew that the massive fissure marked the end of a long and agonizing passage.

She was relieved in a certain sense, relieved in the way of a dying man who knows he will soon escape from the anguish of his ordeal. And so she scraped out a small enclosure from a nearby mound of drifting snow and turned back toward the sloping snowfield, curling up into the tiny enclave as best she could, then crossed her front paws in front of her, gently laid her head down and patiently began to await the arrival of the Mongol.

The storm by now had completely abated and the vast glacial plane that lay before her was shimmering in the bluish white brilliance of the ascending sun. Out in the distance, where Isabel had set her gaze, everything was a blur of exploding light as the sun's rays flared from everywhere across the icy surface. And then, from the corner of her eye, she discerned a flicker of motion far out on the rim of the horizon, a ripple of movement that fluttered in and out of her line of sight like a shadow wavering indistinctly in the light of a waning flame. And she knew at once that it was the Mongol, realized that he had survived the big storm, as she knew he would, and was now moving in for the kill; and so she pulled herself up into a low crouch and prepared to make her stand.

Isabel was a bear and unaware of her own mortality, knew nothing of death as the inevitable denouement of her existence. But she did know that her life could be extinguished by external forces, had, in fact, seen many of her friends and compatriots die at the hands of these Eskimos with their powerful weapons and she was determined to defend herself to the end; was altogether disinclined to passively abandon her existence. But she was weary to the bone and knew it would be difficult, understood well that she was about to die. Nonetheless, she began to gird herself for the final essay, began to reach down into the primordial depths of every resource she could summon in order to engage him; but she was not hopeful.

Isabel lay there breathing softly into the cool air, tracking the dim silhouette as it advanced slowly forward; lay there quietly and stared blankly out into the brilliance of the noon day sun. An absolute calm had settled across the mountains by now and through the silence of it all she could perceive the rhythm of the beating of her heart and it was disconcerting to her, like the slow cadence of some distant drum it was, like an augury of her own demise.

The image in the distance was still vague, a shadow floating up across the ice fields, but it had finally drawn into focus and was constant now, holding steady in her line of vision as it moved relentlessly forward, increasing in size with every tenuous stride and Isabel could see that the pace of the shadow was halting and slow—unduly sluggish it seemed to her as it teetered up the icy slope; still, it kept coming, step by step, dragging itself upward, stumbling from time to time, but nonetheless abiding.

She was too tired to even think about her circumstance, barely able to breathe by then, and while her muscles began to instinctively tense as the Mongol approached, she knew that she would not be able to do anything, not rise up nor charge nor even lift a paw; could do nothing but silently observe as he struggled on up the snowfield, closer and closer, until finally he came to rest not twenty feet from where she lay. And as she beheld his visage, she could see that the mark of death was upon him.

The pelts he used as clothing hung on him like rags and his eyes were as blank as a sea of salt, his skin everywhere burnt to the color of charred ash, the corners of his mouth encrusted with sores. He was swaying from side to side even as he stood there and seemed barely able to keep himself upright. Nonetheless, there he was, not yet dead and still groping the lethal cylinder that was capable of exploding Isabel's head into a thousand splinters of bone.

And so there they both were, the two of them, Isabel the Bear and the fearsome Mongol, locked into a mortal gaze as each probed the essence of the other, both staring into the uncertainty of the moment. The Mongol was bobbing and dipping now, barely under control, eyes spinning back in their sockets as he desperately tried to maintain his balance; nonetheless, in spite of all, he made one last effort to kill Isabel, raised his rifle up to a level position so that he could fire a shell somewhere in her direction, one round at least after all those onerous days of tracking. But he had not the strength for it, stood there tottering and trembling for several long seconds, then dropped the weapon and toppled over headfirst into the snow where he lay for awhile gasping and wheezing, at last rolling over onto his back into eternal silence.

Isabel had watched it all in mute contemplation, too weary to respond really, vaguely anticipating the great roar of gun powder that would blow her life away; had observed the death throes of the Mongol with an impassive detachment. And as she looked out across the dead body, she pondered the motives of this strange creature who had tracked her across the mountain sides for so many days, wondered why he would hunt her down for no other reason than he felt he must do so. In truth, she admired the courage of this Inuit who was laying there in deadly repose before her, blood brother to all Mongols everywhere and half brother to the bear she could suppose; but she would never understand him.

No matter, she said to herself, he is dead and I am still alive and so she immediately directed her attention to the affairs of the moment. She had not fed now for many days and would eat the Mongol when she was ready, but first she needed to rest; desperately needed to rest awhile. She would, in due course, make her way back down into the lower valleys where she would eventually regain her vigor and strength, would try and find her displaced cub, but for the time being she needed to assuage her infinite weariness. And so she

tucked her head down between her front paws, briefly
gazed out across the empty fields of ice sparkling
brilliant now in the full light of the rising sun and gently
succumbed to a deep and abiding sleep.

HARRY THE HUMAN BEING

It would be a long day. Long and difficult. Harry Endicott lay coiled into a ball deep within the entrails of a fallen Ceiba tree, shamelessly sobbing, for he was, he supposed, as miserable right now as any man could ever be. He was buried down amongst the palms and ooze of decaying fern in the dank confines of a remote Amazonian rain forest, besieged by black flies and slowly rotting away, had been rocking back and forth now for hours, isolated and all alone midst the shadows beneath the big trees, whimpering mindlessly in the way of a child who has no other response; for he was on the run, was being hunted down like a wild animal, beyond consolation by now and utterly despondent.

Harry was the reluctant participant in the most dangerous of games, a contest of survival designed by the world-renowned conservationist Alexander Dunleavy. Once a year during the summer season, Alexander would abduct, or spirit away as he liked to express it, a big game hunter, an individual who had achieved some measure of fame or notoriety as a tracker and killer of wild beasts. He would not personally perform the kidnappings of course, rather would hire a crew of professional miscreants to do the job for him, mercenaries who were immune to any ethical implications that may attach to the act of forceful abduction.

The unsuspecting prey was then quickly shuffled off to Alexander's covert jungle compound near the remote Amazonian community of Leticia, Colombia where the bewildered victim was immediately incarcerated into a windowless room ensconced in a labyrinth of catacombs beneath Dunleavy's sylvan manor. It was an austere enclosure, to be sure, but nonetheless reasonably comfortable, a space of some 400 square feet equipped with various life sustaining amenities along with a collection of books depicting the dangers and delights of the Amazon Basin and its attendant environs, an ironic adjunct intended to acquaint his quarry with the potentials of their impending fate.

Alexander was at his essence a humanist, a person of delicate sensibilities and refined social graces, but above all he was and always had been an ardent opponent of the hunting and killing of wild animals. Over time he had contributed generously to the various wildlife funds throughout the world, had labored long and hard for the cause, but nothing of any consequence had ever been accomplished as far as he could determine; and so as he entered into his declining years he had finally decided to do something about it on his own. He harbored no delusions however, knew well that there was nothing much he could achieve that would have any lasting impact, but he didn't care.

He reckoned that if nothing else he would at least be able to exact some measure of revenge, could draw some pleasure from the knowledge that some of these men had at last been called to account for their misdeeds; for Alexander was, in the twilight of his existence, disinterested in the nuances and shadings of his own personal motives. If the enterprise were driven by a need for personal vengeance, then so be it. And if it were but an appeasement of some egocentric perversion, then so be it as well; he simply wanted to make some kind of statement before he took his leave. And as a man of independent means, he was easily able to formulate, finance and execute projects that lay well beyond the reach of the ordinary citizen.

It was a remarkably simple concept really—the world famous hunters would become the hunted and Alexander himself would do the hunting. He would have them kidnapped and lock them up for three days during which time he would acquaint them with the rules of the game, would give them three days in which to both contemplate and accommodate their new surroundings. He would then set them loose into the jungles of the largely unexplored Colombian Amazon, providing them with adequate clothing and a well nourished body; just that and nothing more.

As a concession to courtesy and fairness, he would allow them one day's head start, but from that point on the big game hunters would at once become the prey. They would be forced to feed off the land and live off the land in the manner of the wild beasts that they had tracked and destroyed throughout their years of professional killing—would be hunted down unto death unless they managed to survive for seven full days, in which case they would be set free.

There were no other rules. They would be stalked and hunted for seven days and seven nights and if they were able to survive then they would have won the game, would be released and could return to the life from whence they had arrived. That was all there was to it. And Alexander was fully prepared to honor his part of the bargain regardless of the ensuing consequences, which he assumed would be serious should any one of his victims happen to survive. He also supposed that the rules of his competition were far more lenient and generous than any concessions they had ever granted to the animals they had so zealously hunted down throughout their inglorious careers.

For three years now he had been playing his deadly game and for each of those three years his victims had always succumbed within the first six days. Not one of them was actually slain by Alexander, for he never did have any intention of killing any of them, was incapable of doing so really; but rather they had all ended their lives by their own hand. Each one of them had gone mad, as he knew they would, and had committed suicide, as he suspected they would, each one in a variety of curious and creative ways and always within the seven day limit; but Harry Endicott appeared to be a different kind of animal.

Harry was a world renowned big game hunter, one of the best and surely one of the most skillful around. He was cunning and knowledgeable, to be sure, deft and resourceful, but above all else he was unscrupulous; was absolutely amoral in his pursuit of big game. Harry thought nothing of shooting down an animal merely for the pleasure of watching it die, had, as a matter of record, been known to bring down Himalayan snow leopards solely for the satisfaction of claiming their paws as trophies. He was, by any civilized standard of which Alexander was aware, a brutish and barbarous man and it was with a keen sense of expectation and faint tinge of trepidation that Alexander had prepared himself for this particular hunt.

Harry's indomitable ego had always been the guiding force of his existence and he regarded himself as the greatest of all big game hunters, an efficient killer of beasts, adroit and competent at what he did and very much disinclined, one could suppose, toward the taking of his own life, thereby posing a more serious challenge to Alexander than would normally be the case. He was also as finely tuned to the rhythms of wilderness terrain as any of the animals he routinely hunted and over time had become uniquely skilled in the arts of survival; in fact, was sufficiently skilled and steadfast to have endured for six full days and nights and was now entering into the morning of the seventh and final day.

While Harry lay there in the fetid confines of the decaying tree trunk hopelessly flailing away at the insane black flies, his thoughts drifted back through the ordeal of the last six days. The first day had been one of unremitting flight, a headlong rush through the jungle in order to place as much distance as possible between himself and Alexander. Under the rules of the game it was a free day, a gift of sorts, and he had plunged through the forests recklessly, heedless of anything but the need for continuous movement. The three days of internment in the sealed cell had been a torment for him, a dark journey away from the wellspring of his very being and so on that first day he had weaved and tumbled and twisted his way through the Colombian jungles for eighteen hours without surcease until he had finally collapsed from exhaustion.

He had awakened on the morning of the second day lying face down in a carpet of ferns, soaking wet and aching throughout. The first faint rays of dawn had begun to filter down through the crowns of the big trees and the forest floor was shimmering softly in the pale glow of the equatorial sunrise. A chorus of birdsong filled the air, macaws and cockatoos and many others in one grand tumult of sound that had suddenly erupted from the comparative silence of the nighttime hours.

It was truly beautiful in its way, a verdant, peaceful glade nestled into the chaotic sprawl of a steaming equatorial rain forest, but Harry was quite impervious to the aesthetic attractions of the place at that particular juncture in his life. He was in fact aware of only two things—that he had no intention of yielding gracefully to the whims of a lunatic like Alexander Dunleavy and that he probably was going to die. He cursed his luck and cursed Alexander and blasphemed against everything else he could think of, raged against his fate and against the world at large in a sudden, petulant outburst of self pity, raged on for half an hour or so but then finally gathered his resolve and reluctantly began to consider his options.

Harry had been set adrift in the heart of the Amazon Basin, a vast structural depression of drowned valleys that drains off one fifth of all the fresh water on the planet. The Amazon river, largest on earth by far, discharges ten times the volume of the Mississippi; so powerful is its flow that it turns the salt laden waters of the Atlantic into a brackish slough for 100 miles out into the sea. From its headwaters high up in the Peruvian Andes down on through Iquitos it is known as the Maranon and from that point on to its terminus near Belem in Brazil it is called the Amazon—mighty Rio Amazonas. It is by any measure a formidable presence with over 8000 species of insects, 2000 species of fish and 1400 species of birdlife, a world apart, dark and dense and forbidding and Harry Endicott was hopelessly and desperately lost in the middle of it all.

His prospects were not encouraging. He had been given a pair of khaki pants and shirt, a decent set of socks and underwear, a serviceable pair of high topped leather boots and nothing more. He was, he supposed, at that particular moment as vulnerable as any man had ever been since the dawning of time, unalterably doomed it seemed to him and he despaired for his chances. But Harry had been spawned from sterner stock, or so he believed, was ill disposed toward the passive abandonment of his own existence and so slowly pulled himself up to his knees and began to measure his circumstance.

He was familiar with jungle terrain, had in fact stalked the Congo Basin of Africa near Kisangani hunting and trapping wild animals while working under contract to a large zoological park in London, but he had never before encountered anything like the scene that lay before him. A soft glow of emerald rose up all around him, complex hues of green that tinged everything in all directions from the sky to the soil to the color of his own skin; and out beyond the clearing a maze of bush and vine that spread endlessly across the earth as far as the mind could imagine.

Curiously, very curiously indeed it seemed to him, a massive orchid tree laden with thousands of fresh blossoms had sprung up in the center of it all, a lovely explosion of lavender and white that bestowed a soft elegance to the prevailing undertow of verdure. But in general the area was remote and inhospitable, a tangle of tropical rain forest that surrounded him everywhere on all sides and as he commenced to contemplate his options he immediately realized that he had but two choices.

He could either run or stay put—it was about that simple. He could either plunge back into the forest and seek out the big river where he might possibly be able to fashion some kind of primitive raft and thereby float away to safety or could remain where he was, construct a modest shelter and conceal himself in the shadows, lie there silently and patiently in the relative comfort of the open glade and hope that Alexander might pass by, in which case he could then fall upon the man and try to subdue him with one swift and fatal blow.

And if Alexander didn't happen to wander through, then he could simply endure for the full seven days where he was, managing the best he could within the dim cloisters of that sweltering jungle meadow; and while it would be difficult, it would not be an altogether impossible proposition. It was a stark choice between polar alternatives and Harry intuitively knew that the latter of the two options was by far the more reasonable. Heading off into the dank recesses of an Amazonian rain forest would be a tenuous undertaking at best, suicidal at worst. He didn't even know in which direction the river lay, knew not even if it were nearby—knew nothing, really, of where he was. He instinctively sensed that he would be swallowed up quickly into the somber folds of that forest underbrush, hopelessly lost within several hundred yards from where he stood if he should select the first of the two alternatives.

And so the choice was really rather simple, or so it would seem. But not for Harry Endicott, great white hunter and superior being that he knew himself to be, for he was neither intellectually nor spiritually inclined to hang around in some obscure, sylvan glade deep in the Colombian Amazon awaiting the arrival of a half crazed renegade like Alexander Dunleavy; not in the least. And so he determined that he must set out at once to find the river, must either locate the great Rio Amazonas or perish in the attempt.

For five full days he had slashed and burrowed his way through that baneful labyrinth of jungle vegetation, struggling mightily against the unholy flora that flourished everywhere in that sodden domain—five days without respite he chopped and clawed through the impenetrable foliage of that Amazonian rainforest in search of the big river. And he was not only exhausted but also perpetually soaked and sopping, for every afternoon without exception it would rain.

The dark clouds would begin to form and the skies would rumble low in the distance and then open up. And it would be a deluge, always, a down pouring of rain like nothing he had ever before seen; torrents so strong that they would strip the leaves from the crowns of the big trees and snap the branches from the smaller ones. Cataracts of water would come bursting from the skies and drench everything within their range, soak and sate the land, would wash across the Amazon Basin like some great tidal wave rolling down from the heavens. And with the high humidity that eternally saturated the rainforest biosphere, it was impossible for him to dry out—so he was always wet, so wet in fact that he had begun to feel himself rotting away.

For five days he had slogged through that morass of leaf and fern, not once catching sight of the sun, pawing through the shadows like a blind man. Within the first half-hour after his departure from the glade, he realized that he had made a serious error, surmised at once that he was already hopelessly lost and so had decided to go back; but it was too late. He didn't even know from which direction he had come, knew nothing of where he was or where he was going, could do nothing more then but keep moving, groping his way through the unyielding copse of vegetation, desperately hoping that he might somehow stumble across the big river. But it was a torment for him.

During the day beetles the size of avocados besieged him, crawling up his pant legs and down his collar, dropping into the open breech of his shirt front and biting him. And his head had become an unruly tangle of spiders that were forever swinging down from their webs and weaving themselves into his hair and scalp. Ants and termites and snails and mosquitoes were swarming all over him all the time and it was agonizing, but worse by far were the attacks of the black flies, the infamous piums of the Amazon Basin.

They rose up from the bogs and stung him everywhere in all his parts, teeming up by the thousands, aroused to a fervor by the aspect of his increasingly putrescent body, thrumming and buzzing, incessantly humming about his head and flying up into his nose, penetrating into his ears and down into his throat until he would finally and inevitably fall senseless to the ground, screaming and thrashing about as he scratched away at the impenitent insects.

And it was equally horrific during the evening hours. The darkness was deep and foreboding down there beneath the canopy of the big trees—there was no moon to be seen, no stars, no illumination of any sort and Harry could do nothing more than curl into a ball and wait it out, never able to sleep and never able to relax as he silently monitored the infinitude of sounds that screeched and skittered through the jungle night.

He would lie there trembling, grasping his knees and softly whimpering as he fought to maintain some semblance of sanity. But it was a travail beyond anything he could have ever imagined—there was the hissing of the snakes as they slithered past, the croaking of the giant frogs and chirping of the huge nocturnal beetles, the constant rustle of sound rising up from the jungle floor, all of it erupting around him all night long.

And he was at all times prepared for the worst—a stealthy fer de lance swooping down from the vines, the sudden impact as it plunged its fangs into his neck. Or perhaps it would be a Jaguar, big cat of the Amazonian jungles, eyes gleaming yellow in the darkness as it

sprung suddenly from the trees and crushed Harry's
head between its powerful jaws. Or perhaps he would be
devoured by a band of howling monkeys or gnawed to
death by an army of recalcitrant centipedes. Or perhaps
anything. And so he would lay there moaning through
the long night, rolling over onto his back from time to
time and crying out into the darkness as he waited the
coming of the dawn.

And every morning when the first rays of light began
to sift down through the treetops, the horror would
deepen as he beheld the scores of leeches and slugs that
had latched themselves to his limbs and back and
stomach during the night. They were formless, primitive
organisms, black and slimy, all of them furiously
sucking blood. And every morning Harry would scream
out in anguish, scream until he could scream no more
and then would gently and carefully begin to peel them
off.

His clothes had long ago begun to rot away and he
was mostly naked by now with but a few scraps of khaki
clinging to his raw and ravaged frame. For five full days
and five full nights he had wandered forlornly through
those inexorable rainforests outside of Leticia, five days
and five nights of unceasing agony, until finally on the
dawning of the fifth day he began to realize that he
would not be able to abide much longer.

Harry was a human being and very much aware of his
own mortality, understood well that his existence was
finite. He knew that he would die sooner or later and
also knew that at the age of 55 he was well beyond the
zenith of his time. And so it was that he slowly began to
measure and assess the value of his remaining years
against the pain and agony that he would most surely
have to endure for the next few days—began, in fact, to
seriously consider the notion of voluntarily ending his
own life.

He had battled desperately to prolong his existence,
had done everything that he could possibly do but by
now had grown weary of the exercise. He had repeatedly
tried to feed himself, had tried to stuff anything he could
find into his stomach from termite larvae and ants to
giant worms and slugs, but it was useless. He would
simply heave it back up the very instant that he

swallowed, in fact would often begin retching before he could ever put the stuff into his mouth. His discontent was well beyond the grasp, he supposed, of anyone who had not experienced a similar affliction, for he was not only rotting away, was not only being savaged by the insatiable piums but was also growing seriously weaker with each passing day. And so he had slowly and carefully begun to rationalize and justify the ultimate means by which he could escape the misery of a singularly insufferable circumstance.

His body was by now suppurating with the sores of a thousand insect bites, swollen and oozing from all its parts and his skin was starting to shrivel and rot away. It was an abominable state of affairs, to be sure, but worst of all was the ceaseless drone of the fanatical black flies. It was a constant buzzing that never waned, a low hum that penetrated down through his ears into the very nub of his brain and it was beginning to drive him toward the edge of madness. He would dig away at them with sticks and with his fingers, would poke anything he could find down into the recess of his inner ear to be rid of them, but it was all desperately futile and in due course he finally realized that he was beginning to lose his mind.

Nonetheless he struggled ahead, hacking his way through the unending ravel of jungle foliage as best he could. And then quite suddenly, on the morning of the seventh day, he broke through into an open glade and out in the distance in the middle of it all he perceived the violet glow of a huge, fan shaped orchid tree and he suddenly realized that he had arrived back at the very point from which he had embarked five days earlier, had accomplished absolutely nothing in five full days except to have traced a large circle through the forest. All of the energy expended, all of the slashing and chopping and tearing away at the vines and the roots, all the sleepless nights, all the pain and terror of those five days spent for nothing.

He carefully inspected the scene, slowly swept his gaze across the open clearing to ascertain for certain that it was the same place; but there could be no doubt. He was able to discern the bent blades of grass and slightly indented surface of the ground cover where he had slept that first night, noticed the broken twigs and shredded vines that marked his initial egress.

It was indeed the very same spot from which he had originally initiated his slog through the maze and mire of endless jungle and he despaired, could but sigh and softly moan as he began to slowly drag himself over toward the rotting trunk of a nearby Ceiba where he settled in and once again began to sort through his options. But his mind was throbbing with the thrumming of the piums and it was difficult to gather his thoughts, difficult to do anything then but try to maintain some semblance of sanity.

Meanwhile back at the compound, Alexander was carefully swathing his body in a specially concocted herbal lotion designed to deter the deadly piums, patiently allowing the vaporous emollient to soak deep into his pores as he prepared to depart. He would always delay his search until the seventh day, would always allow his guests sufficient time to explore the exotic pleasures that the rainforests of Amazonia graciously offered up to any who were so bold as to venture into its ambit. And there was never any hurry since the tracking of his victims was always a simple matter, be they dead or alive, as he would have previously groomed the way for the unsuspecting quarry.

Several days before their arrival he would have carefully and patiently trimmed away a small amount of foliage, creating a pathway of least resistance for his guileless prey. It would never be obvious, just a subtle shading of preference, a shaving back of vegetation so as to provide a more acquiescent passage, one that terminated at the glade with the large orchid tree at its center. Therefore Alexander knew exactly where they would be heading, knew for certain from where they would inevitably begin their futile attempts to escape and from there it was always a simple matter to track them down; in fact, in the past he had located all of his victims within a mile or two from the glade, each one of whom had in one manner or another taken his own life.

So he was in no hurry. The desperate course that his prey had unwittingly followed to the glade would take each of them between 12 and 20 hours, but it would take Alexander no more than an hour or so as he had long ago fashioned a short cut that entered the area from another angle. Unbeknownst to his victims, the large open meadow with the big orchid tree had been constructed by Alexander himself in an effort to lend some focus to the hunt and lay but several miles from the very compound from where they had begun their fateful journeys.

He had located the first three within the hour and had been able to estimate from the condition of their corpses approximately how long they had lasted before putting an end to it; and in each case it had been within the first few days. One man had endured but half a day or so, had plunged a sharpened stick down his throat shortly after arriving in the glade, apparently having succeeded in choking himself to death. The other two had lasted a bit longer, but no more than three days in either case. One had managed to snap his neck by leaping from the upper branches of a Maurita tree with a liana vine wound around his head, while the other, a florid, corpulent Boer from South Africa, had allowed the leaches to suck the life from him—a grim death it seemed to Alexander, painless perhaps but absurdly unsavory and he would often shudder at the thought of it.

But he was unsure about Harry. He had always abhorred the man as an abstraction and abhorred him even more after their first encounter, but nonetheless recognized that his unseemly arrogance would probably be an asset out there in the jungle, would most likely be recast into a certain strain of tenacity that might serve him well in the circumstance; indeed, may even allow him to survive the full seven days, in which case Alexander did not know precisely what he would do since he was disinclined to end the life of any creature by his own hand but disinclined as well to release a man like Harry back into civilized society. And so it was with considerable curiosity and apprehension that he strapped on his guns and headed out into the forest.

Harry, meanwhile, was coiled into the darkened recesses of the rotting log, rocking and moaning, allowing his mind to drift back once again toward the past, to another time long ago when, as now, he had been forced to confront the meaning and value of his own existence. It had been in the basin of the Kalahari in

Botswana land, many years ago, when he had been captured by the bush people of that region. He had become lost while tracking a herd of oryx across the Makgadikgadi salt pan, had in that instance gone two full days with nothing to drink when he had by chance stumbled across one of the watering holes of the San, ancient peoples of the Kalahari, a meager and shallow pool of water mostly desiccated by the oppressive heat of the Makgadikgadi.

Harry had plundered that sparse store of larvae infested water, had drained it nearly bare as he sated his considerable thirst; had no other option really, for he would have died within the day had he not done so. He drank until he could drink no more and then rolled over to his side in the middle of the muddy pool and went to sleep, a grievous error in judgment it would seem for he was lying there in peaceful repose when a small group of San arrived at the tiny reservoir hoping to water their animals.

They had been markedly unsympathetic to Harry's plight and wasted little time in venting their displeasure, stripping his clothes and staking him to the ground, face up, legs and arms splayed out to the side at painful angles. They briefly consulted amongst themselves, an archaic dialect unknown to Harry, subsequently swathing his naked body with nectar from a local shrub, yipping and yowling all the while, then abruptly departing, leaving him there to fend for himself.

There was an uncanny silence that hung in the air that day as he lay there motionless beneath the glare of the midday sun, an uncommon absence of sound. It had at first begun as a strange scraping and shuffling, a scramble of movement emerging from the surrounding sands, muted and distant at first but rapidly swelling; and he knew what was coming. Initially it was no more than a few prickles and stings, nothing more than that, but then hordes of large ants began to explode out of the earth and swarm over him, lapping at the nectar, biting him everywhere, armies of them, rapacious driver ants teeming across his naked body, rising up by the thousands and eating him alive.

They were voracious and aggressive and they feasted on Harry as he lay there helplessly pinned to the ground.

He recalled that he had wanted to die at the time, would gladly have taken his own life then had he been able to do so. But he could but lie there, straining in vain against the leather thongs that bound him to the parched earth, could do nothing but scream and curse and wish that he were dead as the ants continued to feed with ever increasing fervor.

He had been saved by the rains, a rare and sudden cloudburst that had washed the ants away and caused the stakes to work loose from the ensuing muck. He had been unable to walk and so had begun crawling and had continued crawling for two straight days through the thorn bush and hard scrabble of the Makgadikgadi, eyes swollen shut, lacerated and bleeding from every part of his wounded body. And he vividly recalled that during the course of that appalling trek he would have willingly ended his life and indeed had tried to do so; but it was no simple matter out there in the middle of that desolate salt pan in the heart of the Kalahari.

There were no trees to jump from, no pools of water in which to drown himself. He was naked and blind and had no weapons or provisions of any kind so could neither immolate himself nor put a bullet in his brain nor do anything. He had tried to open the veins in his wrists with his teeth, had desperately wanted to just lie there and slowly bleed to death, but he had been too enfeebled to do even that.

It was, however, not in his nature to simply roll over and die and so he had struggled on. Then finally, after two days and two nights of unrelenting misery, two days and two nights of probing his way blindly across that vapid salt wash, a kindly Christian missionary happened by and for the next two months had patiently nursed him back to health. More than twenty years had passed since then and during that time Harry had led a lustful and exuberant life and was much pleased that he had managed to survive; but in the remembrance of it he knew that he would have ended his life during that fearsome passage and would have done so without a second's hesitation. Nonetheless, he was glad that he had not.

But all of that was twenty years in the past and he was much older now—older and less content with everything about his existence. And his circumstance was, if anything, even worse than on the Makgadikgadi with the constant buzzing and whirring of the piums drilling down into his brain pan—and so as he lay there in that log beneath the gentle spread of the iridescent orchid tree, he began to wonder if it was really worth it anymore.

The droning and humming, the burring and the thrumming of the insects had penetrated ever and ever deeper into his consciousness, working their way down low into his inner ear by now, thousands of them stirred to a fever pitch by his rotting body, forcing their way into his windpipe, spreading everywhere into every open orifice and Harry finally concluded that he simply could no longer endure the interminable agony, decided that the time had finally arrived to terminate his existence.

But just then, as he once again began to gaze about and assess the scene, he noticed that there was an odd look about the place, an artificial presence as it were, as if it had all been manicured and carefully tended—like a well groomed garden midst an endless sprawl of wilderness. And he suddenly realized that that was exactly what it was, a meticulously constructed tract of open glade that would inevitably serve as a final refuge for Alexander's beleaguered prey, a gentle sanctuary and natural trap to which they would always return, allowing him then to locate his victims with a minimum of effort.

And so it was that he knew Alexander would soon be arriving, knew he would have waited until the very last in order to glean as much satisfaction as possible from his victim's distress; but most certainly would by now be making his approach. Harry considered the totality of his situation as he slowly reviewed the condition of his body—the oozing sores, the shriveled, rotting skin, the thousands of bites and lacerations—and he had to wonder if he could ever recover again even if he did manage to survive. But then he thought once again of Alexander and his depraved scheme and quickly decided that more than anything, even more than the ultimate solace of death itself, he wanted and needed to avenge himself, knew that he must at least try and slay the man who had caused him all the anguish and terror of those last six days.

And so he slowly began to crawl out from under the cover of the log, constantly flailing away at the flies as he dragged himself laboriously forward; and as he glanced about him he realized that his only real chance was to ascend the orchid tree and find a perch, crouch down into the shadows high up there amongst the branches and then pounce upon Alexander when he first arrived— drop down upon him like a rock and smite him instantly with one, mortal blow to the head. But he was weary to the core by now and the thrumming and buzzing continued to deepen as thousands more of the black flies poured and bored into his brain, swarming up through his nose now and wedging themselves into his swollen eyes, hordes of witless insects drilling down into his very being.

Nonetheless, he managed to drag himself from the fallen Ceiba and began to inch his way over to the base of the orchid tree. But it was agonizing. At first on his hands and knees, shuffling forward, wheezing and gasping now as masses of piums converged upon his nearly naked body, then finally collapsing to his stomach and worming his way across the glade, digging his nails into the soft grass and pulling himself forward as best he could; and the flies kept coming, teeming up from the damp earth and stuffing themselves into every available cavity, burring and humming, biting him everywhere. Still, he kept dragging himself forward, shifting from side to side and snaking his way over toward the base of the orchid tree, glowing softly there in the early morning light of the equatorial sunrise.

He was by now aswarm with the black flies, absolutely besieged by them as they all began feeding off the frenzy of each other, throngs of them rising up from the grass and raining down from the surrounding forest; yet still he struggled forward. And then, just as he was approaching the base of the tree, he detected, ever so faintly through all the droning and whirring, the faintest rustle of leaves and then the snapping of some small branches and finally the unmistakable shuffle of a human footfall.

He realized at once that Alexander had at last arrived. He slowly rolled over on to his back and pried open one of his eyes, struggling desperately to draw the scene into focus, finally being able to discern the blurred image of Alexander Dunleavy hovering but several feet from where he lay, silent and imperious, arrayed in freshly starched khakis and cleanly shaven, looming up like a phantom from some distant land.

"How are you doing, Harry?" he asked.

Harry, who was not doing well, gazed up through the cloud of insects and solemnly stared out at the shadowy figure towering above him. And so there they both were, beholding one another in mutual disdain, Harry peering up through the narrow cleft of the one swollen eye and Alexander glaring down upon him, neither one betraying any remorse; neither man repentant in the least. Harry reached up and scooped away another gob of black flies from his mouth and in a barely audible rasp beckoned Alexander to bend down a bit closer.

"I want you to kill me," he gasped.

He was writhing on the ground now, completely overwhelmed by the inalterable insects, still implausibly scratching at his neck and face in an effort to drive them away as Alexander silently looked on. He would try to scream, but as soon as he opened his mouth hundreds more would force themselves down into his throat, penetrating ever deeper into his gullet and causing him to gag and retch. He gestured frantically for Alexander to help, reached out and pleaded without speaking as the black flies continued to rise up by the thousands.

Alexander passively observed for a short while, motionless and immutable, then withdrew his pistol from its holster and carefully placed it fifty yards from Harry's grasp; then he turned and departed, slipping back into the darkness of the forest cover as quietly as he had arrived. Harry at once began to drag himself over toward the hand gun, clawing his way across the tufted glade, slinking and sidling through the grass in one last, desperate effort to reach the pistol.

He was still lashing out at the black flies, still trying to chase them off as he inched his way closer to the gun, scooping them from his mouth and digging them out of his ears even as the blood began to gush from his nose. The heat was on the rise by then and the endless swath of palm and vine glowed softly verdant in the dim light of the ascending sun as the hush of late morning began to settle in; and the silence was nearly absolute down there beneath the canopy of the big trees, deep and abiding, broken only by the hum of the piums as they now began to swarm up by the millions.

www.ingramcontent.com/pod-product-compliance
Lightning Source LLC
Chambersburg PA
CBHW070630130626
46555CB00006B/2513